We all goes
just know tr
There is support on social media,
groups, therapy, friends, maybe family.
You don't have to do it alone. Hope
you enjoy my book.
Saraya Wilson

Love or Lie

Saraya Wilson

ISBN: 979898518622-2

Saraya Wilson

DEDICATION

For my papa, my biggest and proudest fan.

You will always be in my heart. RIP

CONTENT

	Acknowledgments	vii
	Prologue	viii
1	day ONE	1
2	TWO weeks later…	10
3	THREE hours later…	14
4	FOUR hours later…	17
5	FIVE minutes later…	21
6	SIX hours later…	23
7	SEVEN meals later…	25
8	EIGHT hours later…	31
9	count down from NINE	34
10	TEN million panic attacks later…	44
11	ELEVEN minutes later…	49
12	TWELEVE awards later…	55
13	THIRTEEN bright teeth	61
14	FOURTEEN eye rolls	68
15	FIFTEEN minutes later…	80
16	Twenty-four hours and SIXTEEN minutes later…	89
17	SEVENTEEN strangers	97
18	EIGHTEEN hours later…	99
19	NINETEEN deep breaths	129
20	TWENTY letters later…	149
	Coming Soon	179

Hey Readers,

I'm extremely excited and thankful for you. Until a couple years ago it was hard for me to see my dreams as goals. Today I can say that I don't say dream. I only have goals. When I first open my eyes in the morning I read my goals every single day. It took me years to complete some of my goals. There are goals that I am working on still till this day. No one is perfect, not me or my characters in my book. Life can be hard, there are struggles that we all go through. You are not alone. Don't let anyone tell you that you aren't good enough because you are more than good enough plus more. Thank you for reading my book. I hope my book helps you in one way or another. I love you and YOU GOT THIS!

-Saraya

ACKNOWLEDGMENTS

First I want to thank God for giving me the talent to write this book. I want to thank my family, friends and everyone who supported me along the way on this journey. I want to thank Barbara's Flowers in Sulphur, Oklahoma for the flowers to make my book cover. I want to give a special thanks to my mom, my Grandma Dawn and Grandma Vickie. I also want to thank my sister and best friend, Tiara. I want to thank Tristen who has been my best friend my whole life. I want to thank Preston for going with me to Liberty Hill and Austin. I want to thank my co-workers for their opinion and support. Last but certainly not least, I would like to thank my papa. I know he is cheering me on from Heaven.

PROLOGUE

It was a typical Thursday, I kept telling myself that nothing special was going to happen. I was lying in my bed at my Grandma Maggie's house having a million thoughts but all of them were negative. I kept asking myself what I am doing. Why am I here? How did I get to this point? Why am I not smart enough? If it was negative, it was on my mind. Everyone thought I was happy. I couldn't show people that I was sad. If I did show people that I was sad then it would only cause more pain for me and others. Plus I didn't like it when people would pity me. Another unsuccessful day was to come. Another failed attempt at life itself.

I was twenty-three years old. I was dependent on my Grandma Maggie, I must add. I didn't have a job. If someone would have asked me why I didn't have a job, the question would be unanswered. Truly I didn't know why I didn't have a job. I didn't know how to be an adult, it was much harder than I had anticipated. College wasn't what I thought it would be. Someone might have told me it was different, but I didn't listen. I thought that I knew everything about anything. I started to realize that I knew nothing but I couldn't let anyone know that. Even though I graduated college, I didn't have a job nor did I have a place to live other than my Grandma Maggie's home. That morning, for some reason, I didn't feel that great. My body was aching so bad that I wanted to cry. I could barely breathe through my mouth or my nose. I must have been running a fever because I had the chills like no other. I didn't want to do anything active but I knew that I needed to go to the doctor. After I laid in my bed for about thirty minutes, I finally rolled out of bed. I almost couldn't roll out of bed because my body ached so badly. All those thoughts I had before crawling out of bed, stayed in my head. I just didn't want to crawl out of bed. I honestly felt like I was going to die. I never truly wanted to jump out of bed but that day was because of pain not depression. My lower back was in so much pain it felt like I had an extremely bad kidney infection. I knew I had Covid-19 with all the symptoms I had. I was done with the pain of COVID and being depressed was all too much. The pain from my body and the pain in my heart was too much at one time. One of those problems needed to be fixed. IMMEDIATELY! I decided I would start with my COVID-19 problem first. I knew fixing the pain in my heart was going to be a little more difficult than I could handle at that moment. My heart could wait another day to be fixed.

I couldn't remember the last time I had taken a shower. I didn't even know the last time I had gone outside. I decided to take a shower, the water on my skin was just the right temperature. It felt refreshing which made my body feel a slight relief. I used a liquid soap that smelled like lavender with a hint of coconut scent. It was my mom's favorite, I remembered my mom always smelled like lavender and coconut. For a minute I just stood there letting the soapy water run down my body. I grabbed the shampoo for my long jet black, thick hair. I was aching and dizzy so I decided to sit down. The water from the shower was gliding off my skin. While I sat down I decided to wash my face. I grabbed my face wash, pumped one squirt out of it then applied it to my face. I grabbed my vanity brush then rotated it in circular motions against my face to cleanse it. I put the brush down, I looked directly to the ceiling to let the water clean the soap from my face. After all the soap was off, I turned the faucet off then stepped out of the shower. I grabbed the towel that hung from the towel rack to dry myself off. I was still so dizzy, as soon as I stepped out of the shower I almost fell to the ground. I stumbled to my bedroom, I could barely make it to my bed. Once I did I laid there for a while to make the dizziness go away. I must have fallen asleep because I woke up to my phone ringing.

"Hello" I said with a crackled voice.

"Are you still in bed? It's 1 o'clock in the afternoon!" Grandma Maggie yelled

I hung up before she could yell at me anymore. I looked at my phone, I had so many notifications. Oh my, 10 missed calls. I couldn't believe Grandma Maggie called me 11 times.

I was still in my towel from when I fell on my bed from taking a shower.

 I walked to my closet where I picked out an outfit. I chose a Victoria Secret top with some black Lululemon leggings. I sat down on the bed, my bed was so comfortable I almost decided right then and there that I should go back to sleep. Right before I laid down, I thought to myself about the amount of energy it had already taken for me to put on my clothes. I still had to put on my black Bomba socks with my black Nike shoes. I decided to not put makeup on. However, many people always told me I didn't need makeup. I had a soft, even olive complexion with high cheekbones. My eyelashes were extraordinarily long, thick with a curve to them with my crystal blue eyes. By the time I was ready my hair was almost dry. I didn't want to fix my hair. It had natural loose ringlets to it. Usually my hair looked like I used a big curling iron to it. I grabbed my keys, purse and phone then I walked out the door.

I had a 2020 Kia Telluride. My grandma bought it for me, so I did not have to pay for any of it, not that I had the money to pay for it. I didn't have a job to pay for it. She held it over my head because she said the reason she bought it was so I would have a way to work. I didn't have a job yet. She surprised me with the car after I graduated college. I didn't realize that she would hold it over my head the rest of my life. Driving in the car was always the worst for me because I felt all alone. There wasn't anyone to help keep my mind off of all the terrible events that happened. I couldn't stop thinking, how could I get out of it? How did I get to this point? Honestly, I didn't think anything else could have gone wrong. I spent thirty minutes in the car by myself. It took more than long enough but I eventually made it to the hospital. I pulled into the emergency parking lot. I sat there for about five minutes while I talked myself up to go inside. I stepped out of the car. There was a huge sign above the doors that read

EMERGENCY ROOM in red neon lights. I walked through

the big glass sliding doors as I walked in the doors, there was a front desk to check in on the right. While I waited in line to check in I saw about 10 people, maybe more which were likely there because they had COVID or probably thought they were dying. The way society talked about COVID, everyone who caught it would die. All I wanted was to be prescribed some meds so I could leave the hospital. I wanted to be home and in my bed. Unfortunately, I had to be at the hospital for a little while longer. I walked to the reception's desk, built into the desk was a vertical window, and behind it was a woman helping people.

 "Can I have your name and do you have a chart number?" The clerk asked kindly and professionally.

Honestly, I didn't want to be there. She probably didn't want to be there either, but she more than likely didn't have a choice. I felt that life was so complicated for me. I also felt as if nothing could go right.

1

day ONE

"My name is Skylan Mills, my chart number is 647824" I replied with a depressed attitude.

I thought about how much I hated my life. I could have been home asleep instead of being there.

"Can you verify your date of birth?" The clerk asked kindly

"March 13, 1998" I said

"Thank you. Can you verify your address please?" the clerk said selflessly even after I gave her an attitude.

"My address is 314 Andele Way Liberty Hill, Texas" I tried not to use an attitude that time.

"Thank you, what is wrong with you today or why are you here?" The clerk proceeded to ask warmly.

Of course, I told her the reason I was there, while I tried to be as polite as possible. All I wanted was to go home to forget that I drove forty minutes to the hospital in Austin.

"I think that I might have COVID. The past few days I have been running a fever, headache, nauseous, dizziness, and my body is aching. Since it's going around, I figured that I would come to the ER" I said with a voice that was as deep as a man.

"Ok thank you, have a seat please and a Physician Assistant will call your name as soon as possible." the clerk said kindly

I walked over to the waiting area. I tried to sit in a chair where there weren't that many people around. Two hours later, after sitting there for what seemed like forever, I heard a Physician Assistant that called my name.

"Skylan Mills!" the Physician Assistant yelled

I picked up my phone and keys from the ground and walked over to the Physician Assistant

"Hello, how are you?" I said with an ill voice.

"Hello, my name is Jill, I will be your PA. Thank you for asking. I am good, how about you?" The Physician Assistant replied

"I am good, considering" I said with a crackle, deep voice.

Who wanted to hear that I felt like I was dying inside? People only asked a person that because it was polite. No one really cared if I was having a good or bad day. I believe it was mostly just small talk.

"I can tell. Can you step on the scale please?" Physician Assistant Jill asked

I stepped on the scale. I thought to myself has anyone ever said no to that question. Some people might not want to know their weight.

"You weigh 115 pounds" I smirked then quickly stepped off the scale.

"Can you sit down in the chair please? I need to ask you a few questions." the Physician Assistant Jill asked warmly

I was preparing for questions that I knew I would lie about. I didn't think anyone told the truth on those questions or at least the full truth. It's like when the dentist asks a patient if they floss their teeth every day. Most people would say yes even though most people don't floss their teeth every day.

She slid a temperature gauge across my forehead.

"99.8, you are running a little high" the Physician Assistant said

She put a blood pressure cuff on me then pushed a button on the machine it was connected to.

"110/70" PA Jill said

She took the blood pressure cuff off of me then put the cuff back on the machine.

"Thank you" I said.

"On a scale from one to ten, how much pain are you in?" PA Jill said with a smile while she read off the computer screen.

I was not going to say ten, I wasn't dying nor was I getting ready to die.

"I would say that I am probably a seven." I said depressed and ill.

I tried to never go over seven, I always wanted to save the ten for when I was dying.

"Do you drink alcohol?" PA Jill said as she slowly lost her smile as she proceeded.

"Yes, I drink alcohol, but I only do it socially." I said with a kind smile.

Which was true, I would only drink socially.

"How many times do you drink a year?" Physician Assistant Jill asked without judgement with a smirk on her face.

Honestly, I would drink more than a hundred times or so a year, but I wasn't going to tell her that. No one really would say yes to spend half the year drinking. Not every time I did would I acquire the amount of alcohol to make me blackout wasted.

"I drink no more than ten times a year." I said as if I didn't just lie to that Physician Assistant

"Do you smoke?" she asked, still without judgement and with a polite smile.

I didn't have to lie on that question. I couldn't stand cigarette smoke. Everyone I knew smoked except my Grandma Maggie. Even then, she smoked for many years before she quit.

"NOPE" I was completely confident with that answer.

"How many sex partners have you had?" she asked while staring at the computer with a half-smile on her face.

I had not been with that many people. It made me think of the number of people my partners had been with before me.

"I have only been with five people." I said with a little judgement for myself.

Gosh, there were so many questions. I just wanted to hurry up with the whole process.

Then she asked me one more question that I knew she was going to ask me, but I never wanted to answer.

"Have you ever tried to commit suicide?" Physician Assistant Jill asked with a closed lip smile

I was very impressed by the little amount of judgement she showed. I would have put a negative number on the amount of judgement she used during the whole process. Until then I had never known someone who didn't show any judgement. I had tried twice to commit suicide but I couldn't tell her that. At that moment I had to think of my future. If I told her yes, then she would send me to a psych ward immediately if I told her no then she might perceive that I was lying. So I decided to go with the half-truth.

"No, I have not ever tried to commit suicide, but I do feel like never getting out of bed." I said as I tried not to sound like I had just lied. In that exact moment, I knew everything was going to change. I knew that I wouldn't be sent to a psych ward so that was a relief but I knew it wouldn't be the same.
"Do you see a therapist?" Physician Assistant Jill asked while she used a natural smile.
Did it look like I needed to see a therapist? But I couldn't exactly ask her that.
"No, I do not see a therapist" I said a little ruder than I had intended.
"Thank you that is all the questions I have for you" Physician Assistant Jill finally put a smile back on her face, it seemed forced but at least she was smiling.

The Physician Assistant walked me back to a room that was uncomfortable and unfortunately looked like every other emergency room. There, I was, again, alone, in a room that was tedious and empty. It had a sink, a chair, a computer, and four white walls. It also had the examination table with a white sheet of paper on it. I assumed the hospital didn't think that people were sick enough because the room was extremely cold. All I could think about at that moment was, why am I alone again? Why didn't I have any friends? Where were the friends that I had before? What had happened to me? Was there something wrong with me? My mind went back to the description of the room. Why was that room dull and boring? Where was the doctor? While I sat there being impatient in the colorless room, I thought to myself if I didn't have COVID-19, I would go insane after all the waiting I had already done. Plus I had to answer all those ridiculous questions. I asked myself, should I have even gone to the emergency room? After I waited for what seemed like forever, the doctor finally came in the room

"Hello, my name is Dr. Stint. Can you tell me what is wrong with you today?' she asked kindly.
I thought she was kidding? I already had told the Physician Assistant.

4

I wondered if they communicated before the doctor came into the room. Maybe the Physicians Assistants and Physicians just sat around and talked about what they did the night before. Who knows...

"My lower back is in extreme pain and it is uncomfortable to move. I have a migraine so bad that I can barely open my eyes." I said

"I am going to do a COVID-19 test on you" Dr. Stint said

Dr. Stint told me to tilt my head back. She stuck a swab up both sides of my nostrils that felt as if she had hit my brain.

"I will be back when the test comes back. If you would just wait here. It should only be about thirty minutes." The doctor said

The doctor walked back into the emergency room about forty-five minutes later to talk to me.

"You do have COVID. I am going to prescribe you some medication. Drink plenty of water. I hope you start to feel better. You need to quarantine for two weeks. Another doctor will be in here shortly to talk about making an appointment with a counselor?" Dr. Stint said very neutral

I had to wait to see another doctor. It took forever for that doctor to come into the room. I just knew I was going to have to go through the process to go to talk to a therapist. A freaking therapist!!!!

After I waited for what seemed like hours, another doctor came in.

"Hello, my name is Dr. Reels. I understand that you are going through a difficult time and need help?" Dr. Reels said

"I guess, I really don't want to go to a therapist, but I guess I will try it out." I said with a sigh

I answered his questions like any functional person would.

"On a scale from one to ten how sad are you?" Dr. Reels asked

"Do you have trouble getting out of bed every day?" Dr. Reels asked another question

"Do you have trouble sleeping at night or not sleeping at all?" Dr. Reels asked another question

"Seven, yes and sometimes both." I answered

Dr. Reels gave me a business card that had a number on it for me to call. Dr. Reels told me to set up an appointment with the suggested therapist. YES! I finally was able to leave that place after being there for approximately four hours. I walked to my car, I dreaded a forty minute car ride all by myself. I went to the pharmacy to pick up the medicine the doctor prescribed to me. I went through the drive through. I told the clerk my name and my date of birth. She put the medication in the tube then sent it down. I grabbed the medication out of the tube then drove off. I decided I would wait until I was home to take the medication. Once again it was time to think about all the negative thoughts that went through my head every day. All the questions that I didn't know the answers to at that moment. I did know that I was ready to be home and in my bed. I was tired but more than likely I would not sleep, just watch television in my bedroom. Netflix was more than less my distraction to life. I knew when I arrived home if Grandma Maggie was there she would yell at me about the fact I slept late. Also she would tell me that I needed to search for a job. Grandma Maggie made me feel like the world would be better off without me in it. Ugh, I changed my mind. After I thought about all that would happen when I arrived home, I no longer wanted to go home. But then what would I do? I didn't want to go anywhere; I didn't feel like driving home. Since I didn't have anywhere to go I went home. I pulled up to my house, I pushed the button for the garage door to open. I noticed that my Grandma Maggie's car wasn't in there. I drove into the garage then just sat in the garage for a little bit. I decided fifteen minutes later that I would drag myself out of my car. I walked into the house, into my bedroom, I turned my television on in my room. I sat there then messed around on my phone because I didn't have any friends, what else would there be for me to do? Plus I had COVID-19. I was broken, sick and had no one to do anything with. Not that I would really want to do anything with anyone if I did have friends. My body was in so much pain that I didn't want to do anything. My grandma walked in my room with an angry look, it was like she knew I didn't look for a job that day. I knew that she was about to yell at me.

"What did you do today? Did you go searching for a job?" my grandma started to yell at me.
I needed her to stop yelling at me about everything that I knew I was doing wrong; I knew I already failed at life.
"No, I went to the emergency room today!" I yelled back
Not that she really cared if I died or not.
"Why did you go there?" my grandma's voice increased with each

word.

"I figured I had COVID, now I have to make an appointment to go see a therapist. But first I have to get over Covid-19" I said as loud as I could.

I knew that it sounded like we hated each other but that was only because all she did was yell at me. I didn't think that she understood me or understood what I was going through at the time. I had been able to keep it hidden but I thought I had hit my lowest point. I would just sit on my phone while I watched television. My room was big and had one window, but I had blackout curtains so it was extremely dark in my room. I liked it better that way.

"Dinner is ready, if you want to eat!" Grandma Maggie yelled from the bottom of the stairs

"I am not hungry!" I yelled back

"Fine, then don't eat!" Grandma Maggie yelled.

Our conversations were always loud and short. I looked at the time. Wow, it was already eight o'clock at night. I was still watching television, messing around on my phone. I had no one to talk to, so I scrolled through Facebook, Instagram and TikTok. I eventually fell asleep around ten o'clock that night.

The next morning, I woke up around nine o'clock. I turned on a different show on my television. Every morning when I would wake up, I would check my phone and use the bathroom. I might eat if I was hungry or felt like I needed to eat, which was not an everyday habit. Most of the time I didn't eat, most of the time I wasn't hungry. If I could have gotten away without eating then I would have but I had enough problems as it was, I didn't want anyone getting onto me about eating or not eating. I really did not need to develop anorexia on top of depression. I decided to call the therapist, I thought I would go see the therapist the doctor had referred me to at the Emergency Room. I picked up my iPhone and the business card. I called the number on the small white business card, 555-555-0909.

"Hello, Caring Seasons. How can I help you?" the woman on the phone said with a sweet voice.

"Hello, my name is Skylan Mills. I need to make an appointment with Dr. Burn." I tried to sound like I wanted to make this call.

I had to go through a long process of being on the phone.
Sometimes I wished phones were never invented.
"What is your name again?" the woman asked kindly.
"Skylan Mills" I tried not to sound annoyed.
"What is a good number to call you back at?" the woman still
sounded sweet.
"555-272-8000" I said with a mellow voice.
"What is a good day for you to come in?" the woman said
I wish I could have told her that I didn't want to go but I knew that I
needed to go to a therapist.
"I guess two or three weeks from now is a good day." I tried to say
with a mellow voice.
Honestly, never would have been a good day. I didn't want to drive
forty minutes to a doctor's office in Austin to talk about my
problems. That was more alone time in the car that I didn't want to
deal with by myself.
"Tuesday, January 19th is open. We have a 10:00 AM appointment,
would that work for you?" the clerk said with a chirpy voice.
Of course, because I didn't like being mean, I wasn't going to tell her
no when I had nothing else to do.
"Yes, it will work for me." I tried to sound nice.
I was so depressed; I tried to be happy for other people because I did
not want my problems to fall on anyone else. I would just smile
everyday like the next happy person would do.
"Okay, I have you on the schedule Tuesday, January 19th at 10 in the
morning. We will see you then. Have a nice day." The woman on the
phone told me kindly
"Okay, thank you. You too." I tried to sound happy and kind back.
I hoped that no one would call me after I hung up the phone. I just
wanted to lay in bed and watch television.

That whole day went on and no one called me, which I enjoyed
because I did not enjoy talking to people anymore. I used to like
talking to people, but as time went on I just wanted people to leave
me alone. I watched T.V. and messed around on my phone for the
rest of that day. Then, just like every night Grandma Maggie told me
dinner was ready, every night I would tell her I wasn't hungry. Some
nights she would bring me a plate just so I would eat.
Since I had COVID-19 all I did was lay in bed then walk around

about every 45 minutes so my lungs could obtain some fresh air. It was all the same for a week and a half. Once I started to feel better, the next week and a half went by where I did the same thing I did every week. NOTHING DIFFERENT. I just watched television and messed around on my phone.

Only difference with those two weeks was I felt sick because of COVID. I didn't have any more friends so no one knew that I had COVID-19 but my Grandma Maggie.

2

TWO weeks later…

Tuesday, January 19; I woke up, took a shower then started to dress myself. I dragged myself into my car again with nobody to ride with me but my lonely thoughts. I really needed some friends. I cannot believe I had no one to go with me to that pointless appointment. When I arrived at the doctor's office, I went inside. Before I went inside there was a temperature gauge that was almost the same height as me. It took my temperature and said normal temperature. The room was small, it had a glass window to check in at, and then it was filled with maybe fifteen chairs. I walked up to the glass window. The woman at the desk started talking to me. Since COVID began, everything had changed drastically.

"Hello, how may I help you?" she said with a nice voice.
Why was everyone there so nice? It made me feel like I needed to be nice in return.
"I am here for an appointment with Dr. Burns. My appointment is at 10 AM." I said
"Okay, I will check you in, just have a seat. The doctor will be with you shortly." the clerk said
Oh my gosh, more I had to wait. I wondered how much time a person had spent in their life just waiting in a waiting room. I spent most of that day alone, that it became too much alone time. I felt like I complained all the time. It infuriated me more than anything. I complained all the time even though most of it was said in my head.
"Okay, thank you." I said with a mellow voice.
I walked over to the chairs and took a seat. I sat there for about ten minutes. There was only one man in the room. He was probably waiting for his wife or daughter. He looked old enough to have a

daughter. Hopefully, his daughter or wife was not as messed up as me.

"Skylan Mills" a woman said with a calm and relaxed voice.
"Yes, that is me." I stood up with a pleased voice.
"Hello, my name is Teresa, how are you?" she said with a calm and sweet voice.
My golly, I was sick of that cliché question. The only reason I was sick from hearing it was because I had to lie to that person or if I told the truth then I had to tell that person my terrible feelings. I didn't want to tell her my honest answer. It was displeasing to me when I saw people pity me.
"I am good, how about yourself?" I said
"I am good, thank you for asking." the therapist said
I wondered if she was good or if she was just saying that because I wasn't there to listen to her problems. I wasn't her therapist. I wondered if they could talk about their life with their patients. We went back to her office which was at the end of the hallway. It was a very long hallway. Maybe, five hundred feet long. The walls were purple, and the doors were white. There were multiple doors, all which had each of the therapist's names that worked in the clinic
"Next door on the right." said Teresa the therapist.

I walked in the room, I looked around to see what the room looked like. There was a couch, a chair and a desk. There were many pictures on the wall. All the pictures were motivational quotes. She also had a bookshelf with many psychology and counseling books. The good part about that room was that it was not plain. It looked pretty cozy.
"Skylan, I need to ask you a few questions." Teresa said
I thought that I was going to go into the room, tell her my life story then I was going to be done for the next hour that I was there. Nope, that was not how it went.
"Here is a page of questions. We will go through each question together. Each question I need you to answer with either, not at all, some days or every day." Teresa said
"Okay, I will answer to the best of my ability" I said

"In the past two weeks have you felt little to no interest in doing activities?" Teresa said

I decided I would tell her the closest truth. If I wanted to feel better, I needed to tell her the closest truth that I could. Which I knew was going to be hard.

"I guess, every day." I said

"In the past two weeks do you have an abundance of energy or no energy at all?" Teresa said

"Every day I feel exhausted. No matter how much I sleep or whatever happens, I never have any energy." I said

"In the past two weeks has it been difficult falling asleep or staying awake?" Teresa said

"Yes, every day, I have both, sometimes I cannot sleep then sometimes I sleep too much." I said

"In the past two weeks have you felt hopeless?" she asked

"Everyday" I said

I did feel hopeless, how could I not with all that had happened to me.

"In the past two weeks do you have a poor appetite or are you overeating?" Teresa asked

"Every day I do not want to ever eat. Most of the time I am reminded to eat." I said

While all of those were true, so far, I had not lied about anything too bad. The questions weren't that terrible. I just didn't really want to be there. The woman was very nice. I immediately thought that I would like her.

"In the past two weeks have you hurt yourself or thought about hurting others?" Teresa asked

MY MY MY MY, I guess I was wrong, I will have to lie on this one. Maybe I could tell her something that was not that bad but was still somewhat the truth.

"This does not happen every day. It has only happened a few times in my life. I have thought about hurting myself, but I have never actually gone through with it. I would never hurt someone else. I could not live with hurting someone else." I said

Half of that was true. I would never hurt anyone, but I have tried twice to kill myself once in the past two weeks. Clearly, I did not go completely through with it or I would have not been in that therapist office.

"Now that we are done with those questions, I need to ask you some more questions. Are you ready or do you need a break?" Teresa asked

I used a forced smile. Of course, inside I wanted to stop but I knew that I needed to finish the questions, plus I thought the faster I finished those questions the faster time would go by.

"Yes, I am ready. I do not need a break." I said

"Who do you live with?" Teresa asked

Great, that was the time I knew I was going to have to tell her that I was financially dependent on my grandma and that I was living with her.

"I live with my grandma. My parents died when I was younger, so I live with her. It is just my grandma and I left. I do not have siblings or any other family. We are all each other have now. My grandpa died a year before my parents." I said

"Does your grandmother support you emotionally?" Teresa asked

"Yes, I suppose" I said

I didn't think she did completely because all she did was yell at me. How was that supportive? We talked about some other useless topics, which made time go by fast.

"We are almost out of time, so let's make you your next appointment. Is next Tuesday okay?" she asked

"Yes" I said

I didn't know why I said yes, I didn't really want to go back.

"Is ten in the morning, okay?" Teresa asked

"Yes, it is okay." I said

I hoped that it would only be a once a week appointment.

"Alright girly have a nice week. I will see you next Tuesday." Teresa said with a happy voice.

Once I arrived back at my car, I said to myself that is a long walk that I'm not looking forward to next week. I sat in the car for another forty minutes as I thought about all those stupid questions. I wondered if anyone realized how long I was in the car. Probably not, since I didn't talk to anyone, I guess no one knew. I always wondered if anyone thought about me. I wondered if my ex-boyfriend thought about me. My ex was more than likely only with me because he did not want me to hurt or kill myself.

13

3

THREE hours later…

I had driven home, while I expected my Grandma Maggie to yell at me. Of course I was correct, she yelled at me.

"I see that you are out of bed so does that mean you actually went to therapy?" Grandma Maggie yelled

"Yes, I went to therapy. I'm old enough to get out of bed and go to my own appointments." I said

"I wasn't sure if you were responsible enough. Here recently you seem incompetent to do anything that doesn't involve your bed." Grandma Maggie said

"Wow! I can't believe you just said that" I said

"It's not like you have been productive. All I ask is that you get a job or go back to school. You haven't done either of those. So yes I am going to call you incompetent and irresponsible." Grandma Maggie yelled

I wanted to cry so much because the only person I had left in the world thought I was stupid and immature. I couldn't believe that my Grandma Maggie had no hope for me. I didn't understand how my own grandma expected me to be successful when she always put me down.

"All I want is for you to stop putting me down. I don't know why you hate me so much but it would be nice if you would use kind words when you speak to me." I said

"I don't hate you, I am just sick of the way you act" Grandma Maggie said

"WELL, you could have fooled me and probably anyone who has seen the real you around me." I said

"I don't hate you. I don't know why you think that?" Grandma

Maggie said

"All you do is yell at me and call me names. All I want is for us to have a civil conversation. I don't think civil is in your vocabulary with me these days. I haven't done anything to you, for you to yell at me every day about something new. Grandma Maggie, it is literally something different every day. I am done arguing with you every day about something new. We can go back and forth all night but nothing will be resolved. I am going to my bedroom, do not follow me." I said

I walked up to my bedroom. I opened up my laptop then went straight to Facebook. I shouldn't have even gone there. All I saw was baby, baby, baby then relationship, relationship, relationship then marriage, marriage, marriage. My life wasn't going anywhere. I didn't need anyone to remind me of it either. I looked on Instagram and it was all the same as Facebook. I almost wanted to delete all my social media. It was all happy and rainbows. I just didn't know how much more happiness I could stand to see on social media. I wanted a happy, successful life which wasn't going to happen in the next three hours. I turned on the television to escape my mind from social media happiness. I couldn't even breathe without the thought of me breathing wrong. How could a person breathe wrong, I don't know. I just assumed that it was possible if you asked my Grandma Maggie.

Shortly after I watched an episode of Manifest, my Grandma Maggie walked into my room.

"Do you want dinner? I made some chicken, asparagus, and potato slices." My Grandma Maggie said

"Yes, I do" I said

"Ok, go down and make it yourself" Grandma Maggie said

"You seriously walked all the way up here just to tell me to go downstairs and make my plate. It's not like we eat together or I eat downstairs. You could have texted me." I said

"Fine, don't eat. I don't care. I was just telling you that I made enough food for you too" Grandma Maggie said

"Thanks for telling me. I will be down there soon. I will put everything up when I am done making my plate." I said

If I committed suicide and there was a person to blame it on...it would be my Grandma Maggie. After all the rude arguments that I had to go through, the only person I could blame for my suicide in this world would be my Grandma Maggie. All I wanted to know was what I did to my Grandma Maggie for her to be so mean and distant with me.

My Grandma Maggie didn't say anything, she walked out of the room. When I walked downstairs, I didn't think she heard me. I listened for a little while on the stairs. My Grandma Maggie was talking on the phone. Grandma Maggie told someone on the phone that I was such a bad child. She was sick of the way I was acting and she couldn't handle it anymore. I didn't know what to do other than cry. Tears fell from my eyes, slowly. I started to have a panic attack so I ran back upstairs. I didn't want her to be around while I was having a panic attack. I felt sick then I knew I couldn't eat. I knew I should have told my therapist about it but I didn't think I would be able to tell her that my Grandma Maggie had no hope in me. I wished that I could have moved out but I didn't have any money or any place to move out. I didn't have any friends to move in with. I was lost and didn't know what to do. I laid in my bed and cried all night long about the mean words my Grandma Maggie said. I looked at the clock, it was 5:30 AM. I had finally quit crying. We didn't talk for two weeks. Which was okay with me, since Grandma Maggie yelled at me every day anyways. I lost about 15 pounds in those two weeks that we didn't talk because the only thoughts I had were the horrible words she spoke about me on the phone that night.

4

FOUR appointments later…

After two weeks of no communication, the arguments started again. The fights started and ended the same. No point at the beginning while at the end nothing is resolved. My Grandma Maggie yelled at me then yelled some more.

I laid in my bed; watching television; as I scrolled through on my phone. I didn't talk to anyone but my grandma, all she did was yell at me for not having a job or not being in school, or both at the same time. My Grandma Maggie thought that I needed to be in school and have a full-time job. Which I knew she was somewhat right. I just did not have the energy or motivation to do anything at that time. No one understood what I was going through. I did not want to do anything. I was just tired all the time.

"Good morning sweetheart. It is 78 degrees outside. It's February 16, 2021. The day is lovely. You have a therapy appointment today" My alarm clock, Raya said

Guess I was going to drag myself out of bed and go to my therapy appointment. I jumped in the shower real quick. The water felt so good. Each drop of water that touched my skin was refreshing and clean. I washed my face first, it was always the most important part of my body. I always made sure that my face was clean and smooth. My hair was the next important part of my body. I always spent the most money on my face and hair. I wish I could have stayed in the shower all day. I could block my whole life out in the shower. I washed my body then the soap slowly rinsed off from the water. I turned off the water then I jumped out of the shower. I walked directly to my closet. I looked in my closet then picked out a plain blue t-shirt out of my closet along with some jean shorts. I didn't even bother to put make-up on. Then it was time to ride in that lonely car by myself for forty minutes. I turned on my music, I thought maybe it would have helped relieve my mind of everything that I was dealing with in my terrible life. I wanted a boyfriend but what boy wanted someone like me? There was nothing good about me.

I had a million songs on my phone, okay so that wasn't true but I had a bunch. I listened to a few other songs while I took the long drive. The drive out of town did help me.

Last time it took a few minutes to find a parking spot but that day I found one right away. I walked into the office, there was a lady at the window so I could check in immediately. Shortly after, Teresa called me back to her office. We walked down the long purple hallway to go to her comfortable office.

"Hello, how are you today" Teresa asked

I tried to tell her that I wasn't doing good but it didn't come out that way

"I am doing good, how about you" I said

She looked at me as though she knew I was not okay. So she made a warm smile and continued the session.

"I am going to ask you a few other questions then we will actually start with the process of healing." Teresa said softly.

More questions, great.

"Okay" I said kindly.

She asked me a few more questions that were similar to the first week's questions.

"In the past week have you felt little to no interest in doing activities?" Teresa said

"I didn't do anything until I came here. So absolutely, I have no interest every day." I said

"In the past week have you had an abundance of energy or no energy at all?" Teresa said

"I have absolutely no energy" I said

"In the past week has it been difficult falling asleep or staying

18

awake?" Teresa said

"Pretty much the same answer as last week. I sleep all day then I can't sleep at night" I said

"In the past week have you felt hopeless?" she asked

"Everyday" I said

"In the past week have you had a poor appetite or are you overeating?" Teresa asked

"Every day I have to remember to eat or I will never eat. Most of the time my Grandma Maggie tells me that I have to eat." I said

"In the past week have you hurt yourself or thought about hurting others?" Teresa asked

"I haven't thought about hurting myself or others." I said

"Now that those are done. How did this week go?" Teresa asked

Usually, I would tell someone that my week was great. Since I was in therapy I wanted to be as honest as I could with her or at least what would come out of my mouth.

"I did nothing, my grandma yelled at me about not having a job or being in school." I said

"Okay, why do you not have a job?" Teresa asked

"I live in a small town where the only store we have is a gas station. I do not want to work at a gas station. I'm not sure if they would hire me anyway." I said

Okay, so we had more than a gas station but there wasn't much in the town

"Will you be willing to drive out of town?" Teresa asked

"I guess I will drive out of town, but I have applied online for jobs. No one is calling me back." I said

"Have you tried going into places and filling out an application?" Teresa asked

"Every place I walk into a business to fill out an application, they say the application is online." I said

"Why are you not in school?" Teresa asked

Questions, questions, questions and more questions.

"The reason I am not in school is because I don't want to be in school anymore. I already have my Bachelor's degree. What more could people want? I don't care to go any farther in my education." I said

Why do people want me to be a life time student?

"Can you tell me why you do not care?" Teresa asked

"Nope, I just know I don't care." I said

I wish I knew why I did not care. I thought that if I knew why I didn't care then it would help me in more ways than one. If I was being honest, it probably wouldn't have helped me at all.
"We are almost out of time. This week I think you need to work on finding a job. I know that you are going to have to drive out of the town that you live in but do not give up." Teresa said

After I kicked out all the questions about my past, my time at therapy was much better. The rest of the session went by pretty quick. We made an appointment for next Tuesday at 10 in the morning. She handed me a card with the date and time on it. That appointment was a little better than the last appointment.
I started walking to my car. Once I sat in my car, I heard my phone ring. It was my Grandma Maggie.
"I found this job in the paper, it's in Austin. It's an assistant job, you need to go there before you go home. The business is called Everest Corp. Where are you at?" Grandma Maggie said
"I just sat down in my car from my therapy appointment. I will go tomorrow or look online when I get home" I said
"No, you need to go today since you are already in Austin" I said
Grandma Maggie proceeded to tell me where it was. I had to pass it on my way back home so I figured I would stop by. I planned on just grabbing an application then leaving. I walked into the building and immediately caught attention from the employees.

5

FIVE minutes later…

"Hello, my name is Jewels. Welcome to Everest Corp. How can I help you?" the lady at the receptionist desk said

"Hello, my name is Skylan Mills, I am here for a job application." I said

"One moment while I print out the application. Would you like to fill it out here or would you like to take it home with you?" the front desk receptionist said

I wanted to say that I had planned on taking it home with me, but what came out was…

"I guess I can fill it out here." I said

Why did that come out of my mouth?

"There is a table and pens over there." Jewels said as she pointed around the room.

"Thank you very much!" I said

I walked over to the table, picked up a pen then started to fill it out. I was so nervous that my hands were shaking. I thought if I was hired for the job, then I completed what Teresa said I needed to do that week. I filled all the paperwork. The whole time I filled out the application I was jittering. Once I was done I went home.

Thursday, February 18, the woman called me from Everest Corp. She told me that I was hired for the job. I was surprised that she asked me if I would start Monday, February 22nd. I was so excited I almost lost my words.

"Yes, absolutely!" I said

"Would you come by the office tomorrow to sign some paperwork?" Jewels asked

"Yes I will, most definitely! I also need to tell you that every Tuesday I have a therapy appointment. Is that okay?" I asked with hesitation.

"Yes, that is fine. Please just bring a doctor's note when you come back" Jewels said

"Okay, I have an appointment on Tuesday" I said

"Okay, I will see you Monday" Jewels said

"Bye!" I said with excitement.

"Good-bye" Jewels said

Honestly, that was the best news that I received in months, maybe years. It made me so happy, I didn't think I could be that happy again. EVER. The last time I really remember being happy was before the accident. It was nice to have some good news. I went home, I told my grandma right away. I'm sure she was happy for me or for her. It was only a part time job though. I thought that was better than nothing. Maybe it would stop my Grandma Maggie from yelling at me all the time. Then I went to my bedroom, I laid on my bed while I messed around on my phone until I fell asleep.

6

SIX hours later...

"Good Morning Skylan, it is time to roll out of bed. It's a great day to have a great day." my alarm clocked Raya said

Dang, I didn't really want to jump out of bed. I wished that I could have laid there all day. I walked to the shower, did all the shower stuff then I jumped out. I put on a black Calvin Klein petite embellished dress suit with a pair of black Christian Louboutin pumps. I was going to the office so I figured I would dress in professional clothes.

"Hello Skylan. How are you doing today?" Jewels said

Well, there was that question again

"I am good, how about you?" I said

"I am good, thank you for asking. You will need to take this paper home; it is information about some of the work you will do as an assistant. Some of the subjects you can and cannot talk about outside of this building." Jewels said

I reached across the desk, while I gently grabbed the papers from her hand

"Here are some more papers on the dress code we have around here. Also here is a credit card for any purchase that you may need to buy in the future" Jewels said

"Thank you" I said

I turned around and walked out the door. I stepped into my car, turned on the radio. Then, put my seatbelt on. I smirked a little because I used to not put my seatbelt on. I met this older man, his name was Clinton, in the park about a year ago. Clinton was about my grandma's age. We sat at an old picnic table for about two hours. Clinton told me about his life experiences and somehow, we jumped on the conversation about seatbelts. Clinton told me a story that was interesting enough to make me put my seatbelt on every time I was in a vehicle. I didn't know if the story was real. It was about his grandsons and a terrifying experience that his grandsons experienced. Every time I put my seatbelt on, I would think of that moment and of Clinton and his grandsons. I always thought that I didn't want to die in a car accident. Clinton grandsons were in a car accident. There were two boys a little younger than me. His grandsons hit and killed two people. They lived but the police officers said that if they would have not been wearing their seatbelts then the accident might have killed them. I went home where I did my usual, laid in bed for the rest of the day. The house was silent, just like every day when my grandma was not there. I went to my room, then I did absolutely nothing. The most I did was breathe; I turned on the television. I slowly fell asleep. I pretty much slept till Monday because my weekends weren't fun. I didn't hang out with anyone or talk to anyone.

7

SEVEN meals later…

"Wake up, it is 75 degrees outside. It's going to be an amazing day, the sun is shining, the birds are chirping. It is February 22, 2021" My alarm clock Raya said

It was my first day of work but still I just wanted to lay in bed to sleep all day. My bed was soft and firm. The pillows I laid my head on were the perfect type of comfort. I didn't mind laying in my bed every day, all day long. I slowly wiggled out of bed. I walked like one of those zombies in those zombie videogames to the bathroom. I slowly waddled into the shower. I had a shower and bathtub combination. I figured that most average people had a bath and shower combined. I just knew when I was tired, I did not want to step over the bathtub.

My Grandma Maggie was already gone so I didn't have to hear her gripe at me. Which was a relief!

The shower felt rejuvenating. The shower of water that came from the shower head was hot and made the bathroom steamy. The water from sliding down my skin started to make my skin turn red, but it felt too good to turn it to a cooler temperature. I would have liked to stay there all day. The water on my skin felt so refreshing. I ended up staying in the shower for a little longer than usual. I finally had a job that I was excited about. It was a job that I couldn't pass up. The net worth was incredible. The hours were perfect for me. Yes, it was only part time, but I was working for good-natured people. Plus, it finally relieved me from the yelling I had received from my Grandma Maggie. I was an assistant to a man of a large company. His name was Steele. Steele Everest. The building that I worked at was 25 stories high. I found that a little intimidating. I arrived at the top of the building because that was where his office was located. My office was right off his office. I walked into his office before I walked into mine.

I quickly blurted out my name in a shy voice.

"Skylan...hello, my name is Skylan…Skylan Mills, I will be your new assistant. Is there anything I can get you?" I said as I stood at his door.

Steele was dressed in a black suit. It looked like it would easily cost 1,000 dollars or more. Steele had a sharp jawline that would make any woman gape and any man envy him. Steele had these eyes that were between a gray and blue color with long, dark eyelashes. He looked like a man out of a magazine. He had black thick hair that was combed very nicely. Steele had stumbled that was nicely trimmed up. He was 29 years old so only 7 years older than me. He was about 6'3 which was extremely tall to me since I was only 5'2. Steele had the body of Chris Hemsworth. Just by the look of it, he was my dream man.

"My name is Steele Everest." said the dapper boss man.

Even his voice was mesmeric.

"It's nice to meet you, woulddd you like me to call you Mr. Everest or dooo you prefer Steele?" I said with a shaky voice.

"Since we will be spending a large amount of time together, you can call me Steele" Steele said

I tried to keep a smile on my face. I wanted to say something to him about it only being a part time job, but it was my first day. I didn't want to be rude by telling him I was only hired for a part-time position. Eventually, I had more words come out of my mouth.

"Okay Steele it is. Dddoo you currently neeed anything?" I said still using a shaky voice.

Okay, maybe the words didn't exactly come out the way I expected

"Coffee and I need my schedule sent to me today. I need you to pick up the papers from Bessy. Also pick me up a Breakfast Egg Muffin Sandwich, I didn't eat breakfast." Steele said

WHAT WHAT WHAT WHAT WHAT AND WHAT. I was flipping out. That was not how I wanted my first day to go. WWWWHHHHHAAATTTT. What type of coffee? Where would I find his schedule? WHO IS THIS SO-CALLED BESSY PERSON?

WHO THE HECK WAS BESSY? WHAT DO I DO?

"Okay, I am on it. I am sorry, I am a little nervous." I said
What was I going to say...I don't know? Absolutely not! I was not
excited about not knowing what to do. I was about to have a panic
attack in my boss's office on the first day of work. Hopefully the last
assistant left something for me to go off of! I quickly jetted to my
desk in my new office. I checked my desk because hopefully the last
assistant left a note or something. I looked in the drawers. I had
found a piece of paper that the last assistant left. It had everything I
needed on it plus some more.
I was so tired, I honestly wanted to fall asleep right there. I did not
have any energy, more than likely it was the depression settling in at
that given moment, plus anxiety. I was already done with that day,
but I kept smiling and kept going. I thought the job would be the
death of me. I did know that it was easier to go to work since my
boss was extremely attractive which would be an understatement. I
honestly didn't think I could do that job. Should I have quit? I did
not sign up for a full-time job. I did not want any of that to happen.
What was I doing here? I needed to be home. The employees
probably saw right through my act of happiness.
A lady walked up to my desk with a cart filled with mail.

"Hello, my name is Bridgett, I am the mail girl. You must be the new
assistant. Don't expect me to remember you. I won't expect you to
remember me, you won't be here long," Mail girl said

Who the heck was this girl? I already felt like a failure on my first day,
then on top of that, I had a girl who acted like she was better than
me. She better not be an important person that I must deal with on a
day to day basis. I held in every disrespectful thought that had come
to my mind at that moment.
"I am sorry, how can I help you?" I said with an attitude.
Bridgett was very sassy.
"I came to collect the mail. Do you have any mail? BTW assistants
don't usually last long here for Mr. Everest. By the looks of it, you
are not going to last long." Bridgett said

Oh my! What did that mean? "By the looks of it, you are not going to last long." That day just kept getting better and better. If I could have yelled or cried, I would have. I was putting a smile on for everyone but seriously I couldn't wait to leave. I felt like I was doing everything wrong then I had Bridgett. STUPID BRIDGETT!

I was excited because it was finally lunch. When I walked into the cafeteria it seemed like everyone was staring at me. It was like I was the new kid at school. It was terrifying to the point where I wanted to run to the bathroom or back to my office. Maybe I should have gone for a walk, did anything but went down to the cafeteria. I sat down at a table by myself. Shortly a few minutes later, an older woman came up to me and sat down.

"Hello sweetheart, my name is Rose. What is your name?" the older woman said
My first thought was, did she just call me sweetheart? Weird. Okay. So I went with it.
"My name is Skylan Mills. I am the new assistant for Steele Everest." I said
I was a little half and half on this lady. Half of me wanted to go then half of me was happy that I had someone to sit with me at lunch.
"I am an accountant for Mr. Everest." Rose said
I started to notice that everyone called him Mr. Everest instead of Steele. While we were sitting there, I started to think. She knew information on Steele, so I started to ask her some questions.
"May I ask you a question or two about Mr. Everest?" I asked
"Yes" Rose said
"Why doesn't any of Mr. Everest's assistants last long?" I asked
"I try not to include myself in drama but usually the assistants quit. I know Steele had fired a couple assistants but mostly they quit." Rose said
The one job I thought I was going to like, more than likely I was going to hate. GREAT. That was perfect news on the first day.
"Okay, I was just wondering, I had a lady come to my desk being rude about how I don't need to remember her, or she doesn't need to remember me." I said
"That would be Bridgett, she can be too much sometimes. She is the mail girl. She has been trying to catch Mr. Everest's attention for years, but it hasn't worked." Rose said

"Oh okay, thank you for talking to me. I am sorry but I have to head back to work." I said

That woman was sweet, one woman I would never forget.

"You are welcome. I know it is your first day. I didn't want you to feel too alone. I know it can feel like a fish tank in this cafeteria." Rose said

"It is like you read my mind, have a nice day. Goodbye" I said as I walked off.

"Goodbye" Rose said

Lunch was over, I walked back upstairs to my office. I hoped that life would be better, more than likely it would not however, I could hope. I just needed to remember to smile. I kept going like I wanted to be there.

I walked into Mr. Everest's office.

"Steele, is there anything else I can help you with?" I asked

"Actually, can we talk?" Steele asked

I freaked out, I just knew he would fire me on my first day. Terrific.

"I realize people talk around here so I wanted to ask you how your first day is going." Steele said

It didn't go the way I expected it to go. I struggled at the moment with whether I should tell him the truth, or should I lie?

"It is going..." I started to talk before he interrupted me.

"You can be honest; I am not going to fire you on your first day by telling me the truth." Steele said

Then it all came out like a volcano erupting.

"Today, I woke up thinking it is going to be a great day. I arrived here and felt like I didn't know what to do or what you needed. It was like everything was falling apart from the start of the day. Then this girl named Bridgett came up here to give me your mail and collect your mail, she was not so nice to say the least. She told me that I wasn't going to be here very long but did not give me a reason. Then I went to lunch, this woman named Rose talked to me. Everyone around here calls you Mr. Everest. No one calls you Steele, so I am kind of confused on why you want me to call you Steele. I am worried about how the rest of the day is going to go. I am so sorry. I don't know why I blurted all that out. I have never done that before." I said terrified

I immediately thought I was an idiot and I completely overshared. I couldn't believe that I had done that.

"It's okay. I am glad that you told me all that. I know there are rumors around the office that I will fire my assistants, or they will quit. The last assistant told me an abundance of information before she left. My assistants quit because I promoted them to better jobs. I see that my assistants work hard so I try to help them because they help me. I fired one girl because she wasn't doing her work. She would sit around on her phone all day." Steele said

I wasn't feeling so lucky at that moment. I blurted a story of information I should have not said but what was done was done. There was no taking any of it back.

"I knew some information because of Rose but thank you very much for telling me." I said

Could that guy be any more perfect?

"You're welcome. I hope that you don't quit. I can tell you are nervous. There is no reason to be nervous." Steele said

I didn't know why I was being so honest. That couldn't have been a good look on me.

"Nervous? A little bit but there is more than just that." I said

I needed to shut up but it just kept coming out. Almost like I couldn't control myself.

"Okay, is there anything I can help with?" Steele asked

"No, I am fine. Is there anything else I can do for you today Steele?" I politely asked

I smiled and he made a smirk back.

"I need you to organize my schedule for tomorrow." Steele said

"Okay I will start on that right away" I said with confidence as though all my nerves had just gone away.

"I will email you some information. Thank you very much" Steele said

The rest of the day I did his schedule and boring paperwork for Steele. It was finally the end of the day. I picked up my keys and my phone then headed to my car. Once I arrived home, I went straight to my room to watch TV and mess around on my phone.

8

EIGHT hours later...

Tuesday, February 23rd. It was time to go to the therapy appointment. After I rolled out of bed, I stumbled into the shower. As the water that rained from the showerhead, I felt it's perfect, steamy temperature with each water droplet. I squeezed an ounce of shampoo into my palm then lathered it into my hair. I washed it out with the amazing water then added conditioner. I then applied an ounce of coconut and vanilla body wash onto a loofa. I grabbed the towel from the towel rack to quickly dry off. I opened the cabinet to pull out some mousse, then scrunched some into my hair before drying it with a blow dryer. I walked to my closet to pull some clothes out. I took some Fabletics leggings with a cropped top. Then I grabbed my HOKA shoes with some Bomba socks. I was dreading my therapy appointment. I really didn't want to tell a stranger my life and feelings. I snagged my keys from the hook that I put them on then headed out the door. I jumped in my Kia Telluride to head to my appointment.

"Skylan, I am ready for you. Do you want to follow me back?" Dr. Burn said with a cheerful voice.

"Absolutely" I said with a pleasant attitude.

We walked down the long hallway to her office. When we arrived in the room I sat down and she asked me similar questions she asked me last week. Then she started with some different questions.

"Has anything changed with your Grandma Maggie?" Dr. Burn asked as she looked down at her tablet.

I needed to start be completely honest with her but it was hard

"Nothing has changed between me and my Grandma Maggie" I

said

"Okay, did you find a job like we discussed?" Dr. Burns asked

"Actually I did! I started yesterday" I said with excitement

"Would you like to tell me about it?" Dr. Burns asked

"Sure. Do you know who Steele Everest is?" I asked

"I know of him" Dr. Burns replied

"I am his new assistant, other than the mail girl, my job is great!" I said with a cheerful smile

"That is good. I'm glad you are happy with your new job. It seems like you are doing good." Dr. Burns said

The rest of the appointment went quick. We talked about my first day at work.

"I want to see you back next Tuesday" Dr. Burns said

"Okay, sounds good. Can we do it around the same time?" I said

"Yes, so is 10AM March 2nd okay?" Dr. Burns asked

"Yes, that sounds perfect. Can I have a doctor's note please?" I replied

Dr. Burns handed me a card with the time and date of appointment. She also handed me the doctor's note. I walked out of the room, while I was walking out I called my boss.

"This is Steele Everest, how can I help you?" Steele answered the phone

"This is Skylan, I am coming from the doctor. Is there anything I can do for you before I come into the office?" I asked

"Can you stop to grab us some coffee?" Steele asked

"Absolutely, what kind of coffee do you want and where?" I asked

"Houndstooth Coffee. I want the signature blend, timepiece kiss of fruit with whole bean grind" Steele said

I was glad that I had a piece of paper and a pen to write it all down. I wouldn't have been able to repeat his order to the barista if I didn't. I went to Houndstooth Coffee to pick up our coffees. I picked them up quickly. I parked my car then went directly to Steele's office.

"Thank you very much." Steele said as I handed him his coffee.

"You're welcome" I replied

"I just need you to make meeting arrangements with each business associates I have" Steele said

I went back to my office. The rest of the day I planned meetings

32

for Steele with each of his business associates.

9

---

count down from **NINE**

"Good Morning, it's Monday, March 8th. It's going to be a great day. It's 50 degrees outside." my alarm clock Raya said

The two weeks went pretty similar. I went to work on Monday then on Tuesday went to therapy then the rest of the week I went to work. Of course every day after work I would go home and watch TV as well as mess around on my phone. I tried to be positive and optimistic in the morning. Of course with depression it was much harder. I told my alarm to count down from nine then once it hit zero I would jump up out of bed. I closed my eyes and laid on my back while my alarm clock counted down from nine. I took deep breaths in and deep breaths out. I had started doing that every morning to help me roll out of bed. It had been making me jump out of bed faster instead of pushing snooze nine times. I believed it was making my days better as well. My Grandma Maggie was no longer yelling at me in the mornings because I was ready by 7:45 in the morning. That may have been another reason I started having better days. I went straight to my shower. I loved my shower time since it made me feel refreshed. I did all my shower stuff then hopped out. I walked to my vanity to put on my makeup. Right after I was done with my makeup I decided to call Steele.

"Hello this is Steele Everest, how can I help you?" Steele answered the phone.

"Hello Steele, what would you like for breakfast this morning?" I asked
"Hello Skylan, since you know Austin better I want you to choose what we have but just make sure it is healthy" Steele said
"Okay that sounds good to me. I will be in the office in about an hour" I said
"See you then" Steele said

Steele was always at the office much earlier than I was. I guess that came with running a million dollar company. I rushed to pick out my work clothes. I hurried out the door.

A couple of weeks ago I was driving to work when I passed a breakfast place called Paperboy. I decided that day to stop there that morning. I grabbed us both a granola bowl with cheddar hash brown, to drink I ordered us both a cold brew coffee.

"Good morning Jewels" I said
"Good morning Skylan." Jewels said back with a smile.
I rode the elevator up to the twenty-fifth floor to mine and Steele's office with our food and drinks.
"Good morning Steele, I have your food and drinks. I hope you like it" I said with a cheerful smile
"I am sure I will like it. Thank you very much" Steele said

Steele was right. We were going to be working close together. I still hadn't found out much about him in the few weeks I had worked for him. I knew he worked hard and long hours. I knew he didn't have a girlfriend or wife. I knew that he was very smart. Almost everything I knew was information that I could find on the internet. I felt like we were becoming closer. He was acting a little different today.

"Can you do my schedule for today please, also can you call some people on this list and ask them to meet me here at 2 PM please?" Steele said as he handed me a list.
"Yes, absolutely" I said happily
"Also, may I ask a favor of you?" Steele said
"Of course, I am your assistant." I said
"This goes beyond an assistant's job" Steele said

35

"Okay?" I said

"I know you have your doctor's appointment tomorrow morning. Are you doing anything tomorrow night?" Steele asked

"No sir, I am not doing anything tomorrow night." I said

"I have to go to this business awards ceremony. Would you like to join me? I hate going to these things alone" Steele said

If I could have jumped up and down I would have. I knew it was not a date but going to an awards event or any event with the Texas's Most Eligible Bachelor. I just didn't have anything to wear. There went that amazing opportunity.

"I would love to, but I do not have anything to wear." I said

"If that is the only problem then we can fix that. My mom usually goes with me to these types of events, but she is in Paris right now for business and cannot arrive back in time. I don't want to pressure you into it." Steele said

"Yes, I will absolutely go" I said

That day felt different but I wasn't thinking Steele would ask me that type of question. It didn't feel real.

"Are you sure? I wouldn't want to interrupt your life. I know we don't know each other very well. I don't usually ask these types of favors from my assistants." Steele said with hesitation.

"Yes, I am very sure, I have never been to an award ceremony. So I will be delighted to go" I said with happiness.

"When would you like to pick a dress out? I assume you can deal with the dress on your own?" Steele asked with a smile while he leaned on his desk.

The whole time I felt like I should have woken up from a dream. It all seemed unreal.

"I can do it after the 2PM meeting if that is okay with you" I said, still holding a smile on my face.

"Don't worry about the price, pick whatever you like, I realize that it is last minute. Just use the company card. Make sure to keep the receipt." Steele said with a serious face.

"Yes, Steele I can handle that" I said that with a serious face.

"Besides organizing your schedule for tomorrow is there anything else I can do for you today?" I said

"No Skylan that is all I need from you, thank you" Steele kept his serious face.

Steele sat back down on his chair at his large desk that I must add was more organized than any desk I had seen in my life.

I quickly walked out of the room then went to my office. I started to make Steele's schedule for the next day. After I finished making his schedule, I started looking for stores that sold gala dresses for the awards ceremony. I found a few dress stores to go to after work. Then I looked up my boss on the internet. Steele was currently single and had only had one girlfriend in the past 12 years. They were high school sweethearts. The article said they were together for 7 years before they broke up. The whole time reading that article I thought to myself, why had he only had one girlfriend and why did they break up?

I went to one of the stores I had found on the internet to look at dresses for the award ceremony. It was small, the front of the store had two big windows with a door in the middle. In each window, there were two mannequins that wore beautiful, long, glamorous dresses. Above the door and big windows was a pink sign with the words "Looking Like a Million."

"Hello, how can I help you?" the sales woman asked me with a big smile and a southern accent.

"Yes, I am looking for a dress for a business award ceremony." I said with a sweet and soft voice.

"Is this Business Award Ceremony tomorrow?" the sales woman asked me, as she still wore a big smile.

"As a matter of fact, it is" I said with a soft smile.

"I have the perfect dress for you for that occasion. One moment please. What size do you wear?" The sales woman asked

"I wear a size 3" I said, kind of shy.

I had a small waist and thicker thighs.

"Okay I have one in the back" she said as she walked to the back to grab the dress.

While she was gone, I had more time to think. I started to wonder if he was lying about only going with his mother. Did he take all his assistants to important ceremonies? All different types of thoughts kept going through my head. Who was this guy? Should I be worried? I did say yes awfully quick. Maybe I should have said no. Maybe I should walk out of the shop. Tell him I had food poisoning or something. I was not glamorous enough to go to one of these events. Okay it was time to walk out of this shop. Just as I turned around she was walking back into the room. Too late. The sales lady was back.

"Do you like this dress?" the sales woman asked me, while she held a big beautiful dress that looked like something I would wear to meet the president.

"OH MY GOSH!" my mouth opened so big; my mind went blank.

"I will take that as a yes, would you like to try it on?" the sales woman pretty much had to say the words that could not come out of my mouth.

She handed the dress to me, I quickly walked to the dressing room to try it on

It was a long, simple, burgundy dress. It was a V-neck dress that went tight around my stomach and flared wide for the bottom half of the dress. I looked at the price.

"WOW! 4,000 dollars!" the whole store probably heard me yell!

"Yes, ma'am is that going to be a problem?" she asked, still wearing that kind, soft smile.

I held my hand up with just one finger pointing up. "One moment please, I need to make a call." I said to her with a firm stance and a question face.

I called my boss; 4,000 dollars is more than I would have made in one month! I walked outside real quick while dialing his number.

"Hello, Steele Everest" Steele answered the phone with a business voice.

"Hello, this is Skylan Mills. Your new assistant." I talked with a worried voice.

"Yes, I am very aware you are my new assistant, how can I help you?" Steele said with a kind business voice.

"I am looking at dresses. I found one that I really like, it fits me very well. The dress cost 4,000 dollars. Is that price too much?" I ask very hesitantly.

I had an anxiety attack just from asking him if I could spend 4,000 dollars on a dress.

"That is fine. I have seen dress prices much more than 4,000 dollars. I did tell you that you did not have a spending limit. It's the least I can do for you to join me tomorrow night. If you would like, you can buy shoes and jewelry if you want. Is there anything else?" Still speaking in a kind and business-like voice.

What was wrong with this guy? Because so far, I couldn't find anything wrong with him. Steele was successful, sweet, kind and I must add SEXY!

"Thank you very much, this honestly seems like too much. That is all I need, is there anything you need from me?" I asked kindly and more confidently.

"No, I am good for now. Just don't forget the receipt please" Steele said quickly

"Okay, I will speak with you in the morning. Have a nice night." I said with happiness and a smile on my face.

If he only knew how big my smile was at that moment.

"You as well, goodbye" Steele said happily.

I acted as if I was not about to spend over my whole yearly salary. Okay, maybe not yearly salary.

"Goodbye," I said quickly. I hung up the phone and quickly ran back into the store.

The sales woman was at the front desk waiting for my answer, talking to another sales woman.

"I will take it, are there shoes that go with it?" I asked with a happy voice.

"Yes, would you like to buy them too?" the sales woman asked

"Yes" I nodded my head up and down with a big smile.

"What size do you wear?" the sells woman asked

"I wear a 6 in shoes." I said with a smile.

"I have those sizes in the back. I will be back shortly." The lady said walking off at the same time while she told me.

"Okay, thank you." I said

Two minutes later she came back with the shoes that matched perfectly with the dress. She checked me out, brought me my dress in a long bag and my shoes in a box.

"The total comes out to be $4,230.72" she said

Oh my, did I just hear that right? I look at the total on the credit card screen. $4,230.72. I inserted the company card.

"Thank you very much for your help today" I said with a high head and a big smile on my face.

"You're welcome, thank you for your business today. Come again and have a nice day." the sales woman said with a kind voice while handing me my receipt.

I walked to my car, opened the back door, put the dress and the shoes in my backseat, closed the back door then jumped in my driver seat. I turned the radio on and started listening to pop music. It didn't make me want to cry like country music did at times. I loved them both so much, but I was in a good mood so pop it was.

After a long day, I arrived home. Of course my grandma was there. I was so happy and excited about going to the ceremony that I had to tell her. I showed her my dress and shoes then went to my room. I looked at my dress one more time before I hung it up. It all seemed like a dream. I laid down on my bed, turned the television on and went through my social media feed. The same boring activities I did every day. I shortly fell asleep.

It slipped my mind to set my alarm. I woke up at 7:58 AM. Wow! I overslept! I needed to be at work in 2 minutes. I was going to be late. Everything bad had happened to me. I decided to call my boss to tell him I would be late right before I jumped in the shower.

"Hello, this is Steele Everest" he said with a professional voice

"Hello, Steele this is Skylan" I said with a jittery voice

"I am going to be late, I just woke up but I will be there as soon as I can. I am really sorry." I said really fast.

"It's okay Skylan, just get here soon please" Steele said, still keeping a professional voice.

"Okay, again, I am really sorry" I said with a worried voice.

"See you soon Skylan" Steele said in a professional voice.

Shortly after I hung up the phone, I rushed into the shower. I skipped washing my hair, since I washed it yesterday. I rushed to wash my body. I dashed to put on a nice blue blouse with a black pencil skirt. I stumbled as I wiggled my wedges on my feet. I tried to put makeup on at the same time as I put my shoes on. I sped out the door to my car. Then sped my car to highway 1869, of course there was traffic. I tried not to think in my head that I was driving to lose my job because I was going to be over an hour late. I eventually hit W State Highway 29. I thought something on the radio would help relieve my mind of driving forty minutes to have my boss fire me. So I turned the radio on as soon as I merged onto Interstate 183, I ran into more traffic on my way to work but it wasn't that bad. Then I ran into hard standstill traffic by the Austin Aquarium. The music on the radio didn't help me at all. I couldn't remove the thought from my head that I was more than likely going to be fired in less than an hour. What would I do with that dress for the ceremony? Would he still want me to go? It was outrageous. I hopped onto route 183A.

There wasn't much traffic on that road so that made it a little quicker to arrive at work. I finally merged onto Interstate 45 while I thought everything was going to go wrong when I arrived at work. I drove onto TX-1 then all of a sudden a truck hit me. That was just icing on the cake.

When the wreck first happened it didn't hit me until a couple minutes later. Once I quit having a panic attack, I realized I had a wreck.

"GREAT! THIS IS JUST GREAT!" I yelled at the top of my lungs while I hit my hands on the side of my thighs.

Just when I thought that day couldn't become any worse a person hit me with their vehicle. I was already late, then the next bad incident that happened was a wrecked car. I was on my way to pretty much no job when a car hit me. I called 911 right after I ended the 911 call, I called Steele.

"Hello, this is Steele Everest" Steele always answered the phone so sexy with a professional deep voice.

"Hello Steele, this is Skylan, someone hit me with their vehicle. My car isn't drivable. I am going to be a little bit later than I thought" I talked with a jittery voice.

"Where are you? Are you okay? I can send my driver to come pick you up if you need me to send him." Steele replies with a worried voice.

Wow! Steele actually sounded concerned. I didn't think a boss would actually care about my well-being. That was weird. I figured he would be mad that I was, not only late but would be even later because a stupid driver ran into me.

"I am okay. I am right down the road. It's okay, I can order an Uber. I realize I am already late." I said with a calm and upset voice.

"Nonsense, I will send my driver. If you don't mind dropping a pin please. His number is 555-369-2456. I'm glad you are okay" Steele said with a humorous voice.

That was a different response than I had expected, I would have thought that he would have yelled at me at that point. I definitely wouldn't have guessed he would send a ride for me.

"Okay I will do that. See you soon" I attempted to say in a nice and thankful voice.

I hung up that phone call then sent a pin to his driver.

While waiting on Steele's driver, I called my grandma right quick.

Even though my panic attack hadn't fully gone away, just talking to my Grandma Maggie gave me anxiety.

"Hello this is Maggie" as she answered the phone with a professional sweet voice.

"Hey grandma, it's me. Someone hit me with their vehicle, I am going to need a ride home later…" I said

"What! Are you serious?" Grandma Maggie interrupted.

"Yes, I am serious. No, I am not hurt. My boss's driver is coming to pick me up right now so I don't need a ride to work but I will need a ride home." I said with a straight to the point voice

"Okay when are you going to be finished with work?" Grandma Maggie's voice quickly turned cold.

I just knew she rolled her eyes on the other side of the phone. I always knew when she would roll her eyes even if it was over the phone.

"Probably around 4. I don't really know though" I said with an annoyed attitude.

"Okay, just call me when you are ready to be picked up" My grandma said while she used an attitude.

I wish my Grandma Maggie cared more, she never asked if I needed to go to the hospital.

"Fine I will call you when I am ready for you to come pick me up. Good-bye" I said

That call went exactly how I expected to go.

"Good-bye" my Grandma Maggie said

I immediately called my therapist because I knew I wouldn't be able to make it today.

"Hello Caring Seasons, how can I help you?" a lady answered the phone

"Hello my name is Skylan Mills I need to cancel my appointment for today." I said

"Okay, what is your date of birth?" the lady on the phone said

"March 13, 1998" I said

"Okay, I will have that canceled. Do you want to reschedule?" the lady said

"Yes, next Tuesday would be okay" I said

"Next Tuesday at 10 AM okay with you?" the lady said

"Yes" I said
"Okay, see you then, have a good day" the lady said
After   we   hung   up   I   saw   a   man   walk   up   to   me

10

TEN million panic attacks later…

"Hello, Miss Mills. My name is Kurt Busch. I am Mr. Everest's driver. I am here to take you to the office." Steele's driver said kindly with a smile

"Hello, Kurt Busch, like the beer brand?" I said with a slight giggle.

"Yes, like the beer brand" Kurt said as he held back a smirk.

"Thank you very much for picking me up. I hope this didn't cause any inconvenience for you." I said gratefully.

"You didn't cause me any inconvenience, Miss Mills" Kurt said respectfully.

Since I wasn't that far from the office when that guy hit me with his car, I wasn't in the car that long with Kurt. It was pretty quiet the whole time I was in the car. When we arrived at Everest Corp he opened the door for me. It was kind of uncomfortable but sweet. I never had someone open the door for me.

"Here you are, Miss Mills" he said, similar to Steele, with his professional voice and a constant smirk.

"Thank you. No need to call me Miss Mills. It's Skylan." I said

"You're welcome, Skylan." Kurt said with a professional voice and a smirk.

I took the elevator up stairs then went all the way to the top of the building where mine and Steele's office was located. I went straight to Steele's office. I knocked.

"Come in" Steele said

I peeked my head in the door first.

"Hello Skylan, it's nice to see that you're all in one piece. Come in. Now that you are here, I need you to grab coffee for me and you one as well if you like. I need you to call Bessy. Check my schedule for the rest of the day. Print off the pages that I sent you. I also need you to set up a meeting with Mr. Keeling. Are you preparing here or at home for tonight?" Steele asked

Oh My Freaking Gosh! I needed to start taking a recorder in there. It was a good thing I had that cheat sheet that was left for me.

"I will have all the work done. I'm going home to prepare. Since I was running late this morning, I didn't think about bringing my outfit. I do want to make sure I'm not fired?" I said with a shallow voice.

"Of course not. Plus I think your day has been bad enough already. Just don't make a habit out of it. Do you have transportation? I was going to have my driver pick you up tonight if you were going home" Steele kept on with his professional voice.

I wondered why that man wasn't married. He was nice, successful and handsome. I couldn't stop thinking in the back of my head, what were the skeletons in his closet?

"Yes, I plan to go home. What time do I need to be ready?" I said like it was a dream

"My driver will come pick you up at 6" said Steele

"Alright, I will be ready at 6 o'clock tonight" I said as I put a huge smile on my face

"Okay. Don't be late. I hope you have a nice day. You are now excused." Steele told me with a smile.

I went to do all the errands he told me to do. I finished his schedule for tomorrow. I needed a ride home so I did the first option that came to my mind. I called my grandma. I didn't really want to pay for an Uber or Lift. I pulled out my phone and called my grandma immediately.

"Hello, this is Maggie" my grandma said in a professional and positive manner

She always answered the phone in a professional manner. I suppose it was for when her clients called or if she was with a client. I figured she knew it was me when she looked at the caller id.

"Hey, grandma, I need you to come pick me up from work." I said with an exhausted voice

"Okay, where is your work again?" Grandma Maggie's voice turned repellent when she realized it was me.

I wondered if she actually listened to me when I spoke to her.

"3227 Oak Creek Drive in Austin" I said with a snobby attitude
"Okay, I have a little more to do at work. I will be there in about an hour. Meet me outside in front of the building." Grandma Maggie said, irritated.
"Okay see you soon bye" I said
"Bye" Grandma Maggie said
It was fantastic, I sat in my office for an hour as I thought about the way the rest of the night would go. I still had that ceremony event I told my boss I would attend. I wish I could have gotten out of that event. I don't know what the heck I was thinking when I answered yes to attending that event. I knew I would look out of place. Since I was having a bad day, I wondered if he would care if I didn't attend the event.

In the meantime, I messed around on my phone. I scrolled through TikTok which honestly was probably the last place I needed to be. Everyone on TikTok was joyful and happy. All those people were taking videos with their newborns and also uploading wedding videos. I never knew why I bothered to scroll through social media. Everything on there just made me want to die or be more depressed. Too bad life wasn't like a video game where the person could start over completely. I wasn't talking like Jumanji the remake either. I meant closer to the game Snake. When the player had died then came back to life with a fresh start.

While I sat in that plain office of mine for about 45 minutes, I scrolled through Instagram as I waited on my Grandma Maggie to arrive. I heard the elevator open then I heard a woman in heels. With every step she took I heard the heels hit the floor quickly like she was running. Of course it was Bridgett. I walked up to my door. As she walked up to me, I leaned up against my door frame and crossed my arms and legs. I knew that girl would be a pain for as long as I worked there.

"Hey Bridgett, what do you have for me?" I said with a not so welcomed and annoyed voice.
"It's a package for Mr. Everest, I think I should give it to him. It's urgent. Has he left for the day?" Bridgett said with an entitled voice.
I wondered if she knew how much no one liked her or the way she acted. She looked like she came out of a Pinterest office picture. Not the one where the girl looked cute and professional. The one that looked like she was more of a hooker or escort girl.

"I think I can manage. He has left for the day anyway. I will give it to him tonight. I am going to the award show with him." I said with a connived smile.

I shouldn't have thrown the award show in her face but it wasn't like it was her boyfriend. I was able to rub it in Bridgett's face because I was the girl he was taking to the awards ceremony that night, not her. I was sure I would get a kick out of it!

"Oh you are. Those things aren't important to him. He takes all his assistants to them. I have always wondered why all his assistants fall for it. Like I said you won't be here long." Bridgett said

"Here you go." Bridgett stuck her hand out and then she made a connived smile back and walked away.

Who the heck did she think she was? It was as if I fought fire with fire every day I went to work. It only grew bigger with every argument I had with Bridgett. Everything she said made sense. He did say he had seen higher prices. He also had been really nice about everything. He didn't fire me, I wondered if it was because he had bought a 2,000 dollar dress? Steele doesn't date. Maybe he was like Christian Grey from 50 Shades of Grey. He secretly had a red room of pain. Maybe it was just Bridgett finally seeping in my head. I went back into my office after that delightful encounter. As soon as I walked into my office, my phone started to ring.

"Hello" I answered the phone in a pleasant voice.

"Hello, I am downstairs. I thought I told you to meet me out in the front!" Grandma Maggie yelled

Grandma Maggie seriously thought I was going to wait in front of a building for an hour? NO.

"I was not going to wait an hour outside the building, while watching everyone stare at me while I stood there." I said

"I could have let you walk home. I came all this way, the least you can do is not make me wait when I arrive." Grandma Maggie said a little louder than necessary.

"I will be down there in a minute, I am on my way right now" I said quickly, while I waited on the elevator because we had to be at the top, on the 25th floor of a building.

Finally, I hurried and jumped in the elevator as soon as it opened up. I really hoped no one would jump in the elevator. I needed to get down there.

"Okay, hurry up bye" Grandma Maggie said with a mad voice.

How did she expect me to get down there any faster? Did she want me to bust a window and fall from the sky? Probably. That would've helped her life much more. All the stress from me in her life would be gone.

"Okay bye" Of course my tone of voice echoed from hers.

I tried to hurry because she might have left me if I didn't. There has only been one good thing out of the job so far. Steele was taking me to an award show. I finally approached the lobby and ran to Grandma Maggie's car.

"It's about time. What took you so long to get down here?" Grandma Maggie told me with an impatient voice.

"I am sorry. I tried to get down here as fast as I could." I tried to sound sincere.

Even though she would have been happier if I came down from the window.

"Okay let's get home. I have been busy all day. I am ready to be home" Grandma Maggie said with exhaustion.

That was new. Grandma Maggie didn't want to fight the whole way home. That was going to be a long forty minutes of silence. Good thing we had music to replace the silence. The only part that sucked about that was the music she listened to sucked as well. I almost would have rather listened to her yell at me instead of forced to listen to terrible music.

I ran inside as soon as we arrived home because I had to start getting ready for the award show that night. It had almost hit 5 o'clock and I hadn't started to get ready for the event. I hoped that I was ready in time. He was probably already on his way. I didn't have time to let the water warm up so I rushed into a freezing cold shower which was not pleasant. I skipped washing my hair because I can't have wet hair when I use my straightener. I hastened to shave my legs and then I jumped out of the shower. After fixing my hair I scurried to put my makeup on. Then I hurried and looked at the clock. It was 5:49 P.M. I wasn't going to be ready in time! I needed to get a move on. I rushed to put the beautiful dress on and the perfect shoes. Everything was perfect, at the moment anyway.

11

ELEVEN minutes later...

I heard the doorbell ring. I looked at the time. It's exactly 6 o'clock. Dang that was like clockwork. I wished I could do that. I heard Grandma Maggie talking to Steele downstairs.

"Skylan, your ride is here to take you to that ceremony" Grandma Maggie yelled really loud from downstairs.

"I am coming" I yelled from the top of the stairs.

I started to walk downstairs, I first saw Steele's driver Kurt then I saw Steele. He was dressed up in exquisite charm. I wasn't expecting him to come looking like a million dollars which I should have known he would.

"I wasn't expecting you to come as well. I thought I would meet you there." I said as I grinned from ear to ear.

"Why is that? I hope this doesn't seem like a date to you. I think it would be appropriate to call this a non-date." Steele giggled, he didn't seem uptight and professional as he usually did at the office.

Great, that was the exact moment I knew I was falling for my boss. I didn't know what to do about the feelings I had established for him. It had been years since I had liked anyone. I had mostly just kept to myself. Nothing in my life seemed to go right so I had become anti-social. I realized it was not a good life to live but I didn't like it when life went wrong. My life always went wrong. Seriously, falling for my boss. How could I have done that?

"You said Kurt would be picking me up at 6 o'clock. You didn't say anything about you but you look great." I said with a flirty attitude.

"Sorry, I guess I should have added myself in that, I hope it's okay." Steele said with such a perfect voice, with his perfect look.

"It's fine, I was just wondering. Are you ready to get out of here? It's a long way back to Austin. Where is this place we are going to?" I asked with an interesting input.

"Actually, I skipped the part of telling you that it's not in Austin, it's in Dallas. We are actually taking a helicopter to Dallas to make it quicker. I have one waiting at the airport in Austin. I hope you are not afraid of flying." Steele said

NO NO NO NO, you couldn't fall for that perfect man! I had to quit looking at him like I was going to lick his face off. I needed to act professional. I shortly remembered I didn't even want to go to that event.

"Wow! Are you serious? I have never been in a helicopter. I have been on a plane and I enjoyed it but not a helicopter." I said because that didn't happen to everyone.

None of that could be real. It was all so surreal to me.

"Yes, I am sorry I didn't tell you. I thought you might back out and I didn't want to go to this event by myself. I am sorry I should have told you it's not in Austin." Steele said with sorrow.

"Don't feel bad. It's okay, I just wasn't expecting to go to an event in Dallas tonight." I said with empathy.

"Not all the award shows are in Austin or Dallas. There are many I go to in California or New York. It depends on what it is" Steele said as he pulled his professional voice back out.

"I just didn't realize who you were. I looked you up on my break at work. You have been to some amazing places and done some amazing jobs." I said with an amazed face.

"Yeah, if I make a confession will you promise not to judge me?" Steele said worriedly.

So far there was nothing that I could do to judge him in a horrific way. He could have any girl he wanted. He almost seemed like a perfect person. I just knew that perfect people didn't exist. What was it about this guy? Why was he single?

"The reason I work so much is because when I graduated high school I didn't think I would ever get married because my expectations are so high. I want a Christian girl who hasn't slept with half of Austin. So far that has been hard to find." Steele told me with a lonely look.

"Hey, I understand, I haven't been to church since I was little because of some incidents that happened when I was younger. I fell in love early, thought I was going to spend the rest of my life with him so I lost my virginity then he broke my heart. I have been single and depressed ever since. I don't do anything, I go home. I was saving myself for the one person I was going to marry. This is actually the happiest I have been in years." I said

My eyes started to get so watery that I couldn't see. I thought I was going to mess up my make-up. I couldn't believe I just told him that. I had never told anyone that.

"I am sorry that happened to you." Steele said sincerely.

"It's fine. I am used to being alone." I said with a short smile.

"Are you really? Most people that say they are fine are actually not fine" Steele said

"I will make a confession to you" I said

"I don't really think about it. I have said it so much that the phrase "it's fine" just comes out. I don't tell people how I feel because I don't want them to pity me." I said feeling like I was being judged.

"I understand. I feel like everything I said just turns into publicity" Steele said

"It looks like we are at the airport." I said with a grin.

"Yeah, it looks like we are" Steele said with a smile.

Steele had such perfect teeth. I could drool.

Kurt opened the door for us. We all walked over to the helicopter pad. I knew that night was going to be interesting. I was so fascinated by the view I was flabbergasted. I didn't talk much while we were in the helicopter. I mostly just enjoyed the view. He did his job that needed to be done with the helicopter.

We had finally landed. There was a limousine that waited for us at the helicopter pad in Dallas. Kurt doesn't drive and fly everything, everywhere with Steele. I would be amazed to have that job. I wondered if Kurt ever went with him on his business trips.

Like a gentleman, Steele helped me down. It was very chivalrous. I couldn't stop pining for him.

"Thank you, Steele" I said, rolling my lips to the inside of my mouth.

"You are very welcome, this is much different when compared to my mother." Steele said with a laugh.

"I bet. She is probably not an embarrassment to you." I said as I carefully tried not to step on my dress.

"I highly doubt it. She tries to embarrass me every chance she gets. After all these award ceremonies I have brought her to, I think people like her more than me." Steele said he started to laugh again.

I wished I still had my mother there. Maybe not in that vicinity but in that time zone. I didn't know what it was like to have a mother embarrass you. I wish I did, it would have been better than growing up without a mom. Since my mom and dad died when I was younger, I never had all the moments that my friends had when they were teenagers. Even at 23 I could still smell my mother's hair. I remembered sitting on my dad's lap watching Walker Texas Ranger. I remembered all the small memories that many people overlook. I always thought about the moment when my dad would eventually walk me down the aisle at my wedding. My mom didn't get to be there to have boy talks with me.

I tried to laugh with Steele and forget about how I would never have good and bad moments with my parents.

It wasn't a long ride from the airport to the ceremony so I didn't have to bring up so much conversation. Although it was fairly easy with him. I could see how he was a good businessman. He was well driven and an extrovert. He was so easy to talk to.

"Hold on, I will get the door for you." Steele said

Before I had time, Steele jumped out to open the door.

"Here you go" Steele said

"My mom would have killed me if I had let you open that door." Steele said with wide eyes

It was still weird to have a guy open a door for me. Kurt was the only guy to open the door for me before tonight.

"I think you get to live just a bit longer. Thank you" I said with a smile.

"You're welcome. Are you ready for me to embarrass you?" Steele said with a laughing face

"Oh yeah. I bet I embarrass you first. I will probably fall on my face, these heels are high." I said with a humorous act.

We walked up the steps which were small but there were approximately seventy of them.

I lifted my dress up a little so I wouldn't trip over it. As soon as we walked in the building, I saw a camera in every direction. There was a big lobby before we went into the dining hall.

"Welcome, here you are sir, ma'am" the greeter bowed his head as he said sir and ma'am then he handed us an elegant pamphlet.

We walked farther in the marvelous lobby. The floor was an all-white marble. It was shiny and slick enough to the point where it almost made me slip walking on it. The ceiling had a chandelier that had mostly crystals with about fifty incandescent light bulbs on it. On the wall there were people with awards from different award ceremonies. There were movie stars, authors, businessmen, doctors, and so much more. It was amazing. I had no clue a place like that existed. Steele walked me to each picture. In each picture he had given me a brief summary about each award. It was the hall of fame of successful people. I didn't even talk because I was so amazed by all the people in the photos. Under each picture it had the type of award, the person and the year the award was given. I had never seen anything like it before.

"Are you ready to go in or do you want to keep looking at these pictures?" Steele asked kindly

I wanted to look at the rest of the pictures but I knew that would take time

"Yeah, we can go inside" I used a sweet voice to reply back.

"Alright, they will feed us before they start giving the awards. I hope you didn't eat before you came." Steele said with a laugh because he knew I didn't have time to eat.

"I ate a whole cow before I came" I said while laughing.

"I can tell, you don't even look big enough to eat a chicken leg" Steele said

I have a body that most women dream of having or that work hard to get.

"Since this was last minute I had already picked beef instead of chicken, I hope that is okay" Steele said

First, the waiters and waitresses brought out salads.

"It's a good thing I am not a picky eater." I said with a flirtatious smile.

'That is good. I am glad that you are not a picky eater. I would have felt bad if you didn't like meat or didn't like steak" Steele said

That man was a dream. Single. Good. Stable. Independent. Mannered. That guy couldn't be real. Why hadn't he been taken yet?

"No, I love steak." I said

"Good, are you ready for me to embarrass you?" Steele said

"Haha I would like to see if you can. It takes a lot to embarrass me." I said

Even though it didn't take that much to embarrass me, I wasn't going to tell him that!

"Okay, we will see" Steele said laughing.

I laughed for the first time in a long time, it felt good. I laughed so hard my side started to hurt. Soon after we ate, the announcer started to call out the awards. There were different awards for each accomplishment. Steele's award was the last to be handed out. I suppose his award was the most exceptional. That was usually how it went at those awards. I wasn't 100 percent certain, because that was the first award ceremony for me. The only awards I had seen were on TV like the CMAs or the Grammys.

12

TWELVE awards later...

After the awards were given out, everyone took pictures with the winners of each award. I told the people who received awards, congratulations. Of course Steele told everyone thank you. He was different from anyone I had ever met. He was so kind and generous. Then to add to all of that he was attractive. I could understand why Miss Snotty Face Bridgett would want me gone. He was perfect, that was what I thought anyway.

After all of the thanking and welcoming were done. We headed back to the car.

"Did you have a good time?" Steele asked as a smile on his face couldn't get any dreamier.

"I absolutely did have a fantastic time" I said with a bigger smile than his on my face.

O.M.G. WHY DID I SAY THAT? I should have just said yes, I did. I felt my face turn bright red. The good part about that night was the makeup covered my face as it turned red, so he couldn't see me blush as bad.

"That is good, I am glad you had fun." Steele said

"I almost didn't come" I said with a worried face.

"Why?" Steele said

I wanted to say that a guy like you deserves someone better than a girl like me but instead I said...

"I had a bad day and I didn't want it to affect you" I said

I hoped he couldn't read me well enough yet to know that it was pretty much a lie. I was going to tell the truth to a certain extent. Is that still a lie? Maybe a white lie. Which wasn't as bad as a full on complete lie.

Great, I lied to my boss.

"I am glad you came. This might sound selfish but I really did not want to go to this event alone. So I am glad you didn't back out." Steele said with his cute face.

Great, I lied to him. He was being completely honest then I lied straight to his face. I could've just called it a fib but the words have a similar definition.

Whichever word someone wanted to use, I knew it wasn't right.

Dang, perfect boss. That wasn't right, what I did. Why did my Grandma Maggie have to tell me about that job? Out of all the jobs in Austin. Why that boss? Why that job? It was time to give up. Quit that job. Move on to the next job, maybe with a boss who wasn't on the most charming eligible bachelor list.

For the most part, the rest of the ride home was quiet. He nor I said much. I think we were both exhausted but I could've been wrong. I knew I was ready to be home so I wouldn't make a fool out of myself. We pulled up to my house. Steele had loosened his tie and his hair was a perfect mess which made him look even sexier. Steele had taken off his coat and rolled up his sleeves. We walked up to the door, his hands in his pockets and his cute smile on his face. We said our good-byes and honestly I wish I could have kissed his face right there but I knew that was not acceptable. He probably would have pushed me away if I did. We fixated ourselves into each other's eyes for what seemed like forever but it was only for a few minutes then we said our second good-byes. I walked inside without a kiss or even a hug. A short but long gaze was all I had that night.

The next day I woke up. It was almost like a dream but it was an event that actually happened. I held a big smile on my face, I let it settle in that it did happen. I went to an awards show with a charming guy that flew me in a helicopter. It was like a movie. What a night! Now, I have to wake up tomorrow to go to a job to see my mesmeric boss. I pretty much needed to act as though the night before didn't happen. No one knew the feelings I had for him. No one knew the connection we had that night. I woke up like I did every morning then I had the thought of not doing anything that day. Even though my boss was out of this world, amazing. Every time I saw him, I lost my breath. I walked to the bathroom to turn the water on. I let the water warm up before I dragged myself in the shower. After I dragged myself in the shower, I felt the warmth of the water sliding down my body. I made a circle rotation to clean my body with a loofah which was relaxing and soothing. Every drop of water that hit me felt better, I didn't want to get out of the shower. In there, life felt as if it were at a standstill. Even though I knew it had not stopped, in that moment time had stopped, everything outside of there was gone for a short minute. No allured boss for me to worry that I would jump his bones; not dealing with a grandma who yelled at me all the time. Not one complication in life at that moment. It was just me and the shower.

I stepped out of the shower and dried my body off. I rolled my hair in a towel. I went back to my room to put on clothes and there was a start to another day. Another day I was going to have to see freaking Bridgett. I wondered why that woman couldn't quit or find interest in someone else. Clearly he didn't see her as anything but a mail girl. Stupid Bridgett. After I had all those terrible thoughts about Bridgett while I was getting ready for work. I decided I didn't feel like going to work. For a moment I thought I should call into work. I honestly considered calling into work. Some people I just couldn't handle, she was one of those people. Dang that Bridgett! I hated that I had to go to work to see her. Shortly after I thought about it, I decided I wouldn't go into work.

"Hey, I am sorry but I can't make it to work today. I am not feeling well." I tried to sound sick but I didn't think it would work or not. Surprisingly, it did!

"Do you have food poisoning? I hope you didn't catch something from last night? Do you need anything?" Steele said worried

"No, I will be fine. I don't know what it is, I should be back at work tomorrow." I said as I tried to sound sick. I realized that I was not supposed to be calling into work that early into a job.

"I hope you start to feel better. I will see you tomorrow." Steele said very professional and sincere.

For the rest of that day, I stayed in bed. I had blackout curtains so my room was very dark, just the way I liked it! I could have slept all day if my Grandma Maggie would have allowed me to sleep all day. It was so much better that way. I knew she would come home early to see I was not at work. Then, of course she would yell at me then nonsense would start. Grandma Maggie would probably tell me I was fired because I just started that job. I called in so that was that. Nothing was going to change it now. I doubt he would fire me. If he did then oh well.

Grandma Maggie walked into my room just like I had expected.

"I called into work today, just to inform you" I said

"ARE YOU KIDDING ME!" Grandma Maggie yelled

"Nope, I am dead serious" I said quietly with my eyes still closed.

I already knew what she was talking about so it wasn't like I needed to ask.

"What is your excuse?" Grandma Maggie said

"I didn't feel good. Is that good enough for you? It was good enough for Mr. Everest" I said quietly.

I wanted to jump up and yell at the same time I wanted to go back to sleep. I wondered what time it was?

"If you do not start going to work, I am going to make you move out. I am sick of this behavior Skylan" Grandma Maggie finally quit yelling, I wasn't sure if that was good or bad.

"You wouldn't. We only have each other." I rolled over and yelled.

That brought back the memory of when I was told that my parents were dead. It was the hardest experience that I had gone through as a child. I wouldn't wish that upon my worst enemy. My Grandma Maggie sat me down at what was my home at the time. Since I was so young she just told me at that time my parents were never coming home. She told me I would be moving in with her. Grandma Maggie said it would be like when grandpa went away but he was always watching over us. Not until I was older did I know what "never coming back or going away" meant. I could not tell a kid that their parents are dead even if the child understood what it meant. One parent was hard but both. When I think back, I remember us as the perfect family. My parents were always kind and caring to one another. When I think of a man I want to marry, I think of the way my father treated my mother.

One day, they are driving in a car then the next moment a drunk driver hits them. How could someone drink then hop in a car to drive with the chance that person could kill someone? I didn't drink and drive because my parents were killed that way. It always haunted me. My Grandma Maggie didn't even know what I felt like back then or even now. All she did was yell at me about every little mess up I did. I just didn't have the desire to do anything. I didn't know if it was actually because she yelled at me or if it was something else. All I knew was I didn't want to do anything anymore. It seemed like it was all a waste of time. Since I started that job with a cute guy as my boss, it gave me a little more motivation to roll out of bed. It just wasn't enough motivation for that whole day. It almost felt like the night before wore me out so much that I didn't want to do anything the next day, maybe the rest of the week.

I guessed it was about 5 o'clock in the afternoon. She usually clocked out at 4 o'clock then pulled into the garage around 5 PM, either way, that day wasn't over yet. I didn't sleep much but hopefully I wouldn't be up all night. That was usually how it went. I would sleep all day then stay up all night. I didn't usually have the energy to do anything at night, I just couldn't sleep. I usually would watch television while I scrolled on TikTok until I fell asleep. Even though I slept all day, I was still extremely tired. I didn't really know what to do about it.

How could I consistently be tired all the time even though I had slept for over eight hours? It didn't make any sense to me. I wished I had the energy and motivation that other people had, most girls my age were filled with happiness and energy like the Energizer Bunny. Girls my age all lived their perfect life while I was always tired with no beauty or energy in my life.

13

THIRTEEN bright teeth later...

KNOCK KNOCK

Seriously, was there someone at the door? Who would show up at the house at 5:30 at night? I bet it was another friend of Grandma Maggie's. She had more of a life than I did and she was sixty-seven. How in the world could that be possible? She usually warned me if someone was coming over. Maybe it escaped her mind or she decided just not to tell me. I walked to the edge of the stairs and saw him.

"Hello Mr. Everest, would you like to come in?" Grandma Maggie said in such kind words.

"Thank you very much, Skylan said she was sick. My mother taught me how to cook so I thought I would bring her some homemade soup. One of her recipes is homemade chicken noodle soup. I wanted to bring some for her to eat so hopefully it will make her feel better. I wasn't sure if it was my fault from last night or not. If she is asleep, I don't want to wake her. I am sorry I didn't call first. I should have called" Steele said very softly.

Steele went all the way to Liberty Hill to take me homemade chicken noodle soup. YOU HAD TO BE FREAKING KIDDING ME! OMG!

Great! He was sweet. He knew how to cook. He was smart. He was wealthy. Was he Superman too? It was ridiculous the amount of talent I saw in him.

"It's fine. You may come in if you like. I will take this to the kitchen, she can eat some when she wakes up." Grandma Maggie said with a smile.

"Thank you very much. Thank you for inviting me into your home. Again, I am sorry that I didn't call before showing up. I made extra so you could have some too. I wasn't sure if you were sick as well." Steele said with such deep sympathy.

I almost walked downstairs to tell him thank you. I couldn't believe he brought me homemade chicken noodle soup. I wanted to tell him he was sweet for bringing me homemade soup. But, I didn't because I highly doubt I looked sick. I wasn't going to lose my job overlooking healthy. So I ended up not going downstairs.

"If you ever need anything, tell Skylan and we will do our best to help you out." Grandma Maggie said with a big smile.

I bet she was smiling because he was so cute. He looked good in pictures but there was no comparison to real life.

"Okay, well I am sorry I have to run but I have church at 6:30. Hopefully I am not late. Thank you for accepting the chicken noodle soup and inviting me into your home. I hope that Miss Mills starts to feel better. Let me know if either one of you needs anything." Steele said with a perfect smile.

Why was he so kind, charming and perfect? I wondered why he was doing that. What person would do all those kind gestures for their own assistant? I wasn't sure, it was weird. How did he have time to go to church and run a huge company? I grew up in church but the older I became the less I wanted to go. It was around the time I quit going to church, I just wanted to hang out with my friends. We all grew up in church but we cared about other activities more. Plus after my parents died, it was hard for me to go to church. How could God take parents away from a young girl?

"Thank you very much" Grandma Maggie said

"You and your granddaughter are more than welcome to come to church anytime. I go every Sunday and Wednesday." Steele said while he walked out the door.

"Thank you, we might take you up on your offer sometime." Grandma Maggie said

"Thanks Grandma Maggie that was exactly what I did not want you to say" I said quietly.

"Have a nice night" Steele said

"You as well" Grandma Maggie said

She shut the door while they both waved with big smiles on their faces

When I was little, my parents took me to church every Sunday. Then the accident happened. Everyone that I had grown up with had known my story. I was the girl whose parents died in the car accident by a drunk driver going into Austin. It was my parent's anniversary. They were the perfect couple. About a year after it happened, Grandma Maggie started to tell me stories about them. The stories were like listening to fairy tales. As a little girl I always hoped I would have a marriage like theirs. She told me the stories for about six months then she quit talking about my parents all together. My Grandma Maggie hasn't said anything about my parents in years.

"YOUR BOSS BROUGHT YOU HOMEMADE CHICKEN NOODLE SOUP. I KNOW YOU ARE NOT SICK BUT IF YOU WANT ANY YOU CAN COME DOWN HERE AND MAKE IT YOURSELF. YOU SHOULDN'T HAVE CALLED IN TODAY!" Grandma Maggie yelled from the bottom of the stairs.

"Fine" I yelled back while I was walking back to my room.

I never understood her, why did she act like that? I wished we were closer like normal grandchildren were with their grandparents. My grandpa died about a year before my parents. I honestly think that

Grandma Maggie was still trying to heal from that when my parents died.

I craved some of that soup but I wasn't hungry enough to walk downstairs to see her. I decided to wait till Grandma Maggie went to bed. I figured it wouldn't take long for me to want her to hurry to bed. I was very curious about that chicken noodle soup. I wondered if Grandma Maggie ate any of the soup. It was homemade so who wouldn't want some.

I went into my room then fell asleep. I woke up around 10PM. I immediately went downstairs to make a bowl of soup. Grandma Maggie usually was in bed by 9:30 at night so I figured she wouldn't be up. Of course the night I went downstairs, she was still downstairs reading her book. I quickly and quietly tried to go to the kitchen without her seeing me. I should have known she has eyes all around her.

"You are finally coming down to make a bowl of chicken noodle soup. You should have come down when he was here?" Grandma Maggie said still looking at her book, not yelling

"Yes, I figured you would be asleep by now" I said

"I zoned into my book that I didn't realize it was already 10PM. That soup is in the refrigerator" said Grandma Maggie

"Alright, thanks. Goodnight" I said

"Night" Grandma Maggie said

Even though it wasn't yelling, it was a short conversation. I walked into the kitchen to make some soup then headed back upstairs. By the time I had come back through the living room she was already upstairs in bed. So I decided to stay downstairs and watch television.

While I watched TV, I ate my soup. When I was younger my mom made me homemade chicken noodle soup. It was really good, I could still taste it when I thought about chicken noodle soup.

I picked up the bowl, then took it to the kitchen. I sat it down on the counter then headed back up the stairs to my room.

I walked back to my room, I picked up my phone to check it. Of course I didn't have any notifications. I set my alarm for the next morning. I laid down on my bed then fell asleep right away.

Fantastic, it was Thursday. Just as amazing as yesterday was, I knew I had to go back to work that day. I did the same thing I did every morning. I rolled over to hit snooze about 20 times before I actually rolled out of bed. I walked to my bathroom and hopped in the shower. Like every morning I wished I could've stayed in the shower all day.

I wanted to talk to my mom so bad that day. Even if it was just for a short moment. I could've used some mother/daughter time that day. Then I remembered I didn't have a car.

OH MY GOSH!

I hoped my Grandma Maggie hadn't left for work yet. I jumped out of the shower then I put my robe on then ran downstairs. As soon as I saw her in the kitchen, my heartbeat immediately went back to normal.

"Hey grandma, I need a ride to work please" I said

"It's the reason I am still here. You are going to work today. I knew you were going to need a ride to work today. I remember what happened to the car that is no longer in my driveway" Grandma Maggie said

"I just came down here to ask for a ride" I said

"Okay, you better be ready in ten minutes because I am leaving to go to the office whether you are in the car or not. I already called my work to tell them I am going to be late because you were in a wreck. I don't want to be later than I need to be. So ten minutes." Grandma Maggie said

How did I always end up in a fight with her?

"Seriously, it is going to take me at least twenty minutes for me to appear ready. My hair is wet plus I still need to put make-up on as well as clothes." I said

"Whatever, I don't want to fight with you this morning. Just go finish looking as though you want to appear at work. I don't want to be late for my job." Grandma Maggie said

I ran upstairs in a dash to appear ready for work. I grabbed the blow dryer to blow dry my hair. I honestly didn't want to do anything. I would have rather laid in bed but in exchange I was yelled at for skipping work by my Grandma Maggie. The arguments and bitterness that seemed to go on between us was outrageous. It was so loud that I was sure people down the block could hear us.

I tried to rush to put my make-up on but that was hard to do. I put foundation, powder, and blush on which didn't take that long but my mascara always took the longest. The whole time I was applying my makeup on I kept one thought on my mind, the ride to work wasn't going to be fun. It was either going to be an awkward quiet or it would be filled with arguments. Either way it went, I wasn't excited for either outcome.

I walked down the stairs. The loud voice from her mouth had already started because I took 20 minutes instead of 10 minutes. I told her it would take more than 10 minutes.

"Hurry up, hurry up we need to leave" Grandma Maggie said

"I am trying, I have to be at work too" I said

We both headed out the door. I ran to the car, she slowly walked to the car. Both of us looked at the time as soon as we gathered in the car.

"See we are both going to be late because you had to take twenty minutes to appear ready for work. We better not have to wait too long for traffic driving into Austin. It's a good thing we both work in Austin today. I am going to contact the insurance company to rent you a rental car today. I refuse to drive you every day." Grandma Maggie yelled while she moved her hand around.

I was about to put AirPods in so I didn't have to listen to her.

"I know you want to yell at me about everything I do but I just want to go to work. Can we please just drive to work without saying a word?" I asked kindly.

I just didn't want to argue this morning. I wish I could ride to work with someone who didn't yell at me about everything I did wrong.

"I guess, you are going to put your AirPods in anyway." Grandma Maggie said

"Correct, you already know what is going to happen so why are you outraged right now?" I said

My Grandma Maggie knew I was sick of hearing her yell at me. I figured she would start to accept the hint that I did not want to listen or argue with her. For the rest of the time in the car I listened to my music. Just like we expected, we arrived at a standstill, complete stop in traffic on our way into Austin. I just listened to my music and let her drive. Grandma Maggie didn't like it but I put my feet on the dash. I didn't want to start any fights about her driving. She wasn't the best driver in the world but she was hardheaded. She would probably have said the same about me.

Finally, we arrived at my work. Grandma Maggie dropped me off at the front door. I walked in and saw Jewels.

14

FOURTEEN eye rolls later...

"Good morning, how are you doing?" Jewels asked and smiled.

"I'm doing good, how about you?" I said

"I'm good. Here are some papers for Mr. Everest" Jewels said

I grabbed the papers from Jewels then went to the elevator.

As soon as the elevator door opened I saw Bridgett and some other person I didn't know. Of course Bridgett had to put her input out there.

"Hello, I thought since you were gone yesterday that you weren't coming back but you are still here? Are you trying to beat the record?" Bridgett laughed.

"You have to be kidding me" I said with a low voice.

"I'm sorry I didn't hear you?" Bridgett said with a snobby attitude.

I knew the guy in the elevator had listened to the whole conversation because at one point I saw him roll his eyes.

"I'm not sure what your problem is with me but I have done nothing wrong to you. Stop with this attitude, I don't have time for it" I said discourteously.

"What is wrong with you today?" Bridgett asked

"Nothing is wrong with me. I'm just sick of your abrupt personality. You manage to irritate everyone here...if you didn't know" I said

I almost felt like I was living in high school. I knew what I said was rude but I was not going to deal with that every morning. Especially that morning, the problems I had going on in my life plus my grandma had to drive me to work. Who wants their grandparent driving them to work when they are old enough to drive themselves? NO ONE. Then we had Bridgett, who was like the popular pretty bully everyone wanted to look like but secretly hated her because she was a pesticide.

"You are just exaggerating. I am very kind and you are the person who is being rude. I have done nothing to you." Bridgett said

"You have to be kidding me. Since my first day you have told me I was going to be fired." I said while rolling my eyes.

"And there are reasons behind everything I have said to you up until this moment. I have been here for years. I know information that no one knows here. I know more than you can ever imagine so yes, you will be fired soon or quit" Bridgett said

Part of me wanted to believe her. What if there was information that I needed to know that she knew. I wondered if the information she knew was about Steele or was about the company. What was the information that she knew? I knew it was mean but she was only the mail girl. Maybe she did have an abundance of information on this company or the people in the building.

"Would you care to fill me in, since you know so much?" I said with a sassy attitude.

"Nope, I had to figure it out on my own so can you, if you are here long enough." Bridget said

"Fine whatever, I will be here long enough to find out everything you know and more." I said

Girls like Bridgett ran my blood pressure through the roof. I couldn't fathom how much she made me want to yell at the top of my lungs at her.

I hadn't done anything to that girl but she was extremely adamant to bring me down, I didn't understand.

"Alright, we will see" Bridgett said as she walked out of the elevator.

"We will" I yelled

"You will what?" Steele said

"Nothing, I was talking to Bridgett about girl stuff" I said

"Great, I am glad you are making friends" Steele said

"Yeah...it's great" I said with a fake smile.

Men are oblivious to everything. Girl stuff. Really. Bridgett and I, friends? Nope. Not really. I did wish she would have told me about what happened around here. I knew that was gossip. I shouldn't be interested but seriously, what if it was something I should have known.

"Do you need anything sir?" I said

"Yes, actually I do. I need you to make 12,000 copies of the pages I am going to send you in about thirty minutes." Steele said

"Anything else you need me to do" I said

"Did you manage to find a rental while your car is being fixed?" Steele said

"No, that is going to be taken care of today" I said

"So how did you arrive at work? I am famished, I didn't stop by to grab any breakfast this morning. Did you?" Steele said

"I am sorry. My grandma drove me to work so I didn't stop by and grab you breakfast." I said

"It's alright, take the car to go grab us some breakfast. I need something healthy. There is a restaurant called The Steeping Room. I will email you my order." Steele said

"Okay, I will be right back. Anything else?" I said

I hoped there was nothing else. 12,000 copies. That was a bunch of paper

"Nope that is all" Steele said

I tried to keep in mind that I need to pay attention to him. I needed to figure out what was wrong with him. So far, he hasn't sounded like a serial killer. 12,000 copies. That was one of my funniest projects I have ever done.

I picked up my purse then headed to the elevator.

Kurt was waiting in front of the building. Steele must have told him.

"Kurt, do you know the healthy breakfast place Steele wants me to go to?" I ask

"Yes Miss Mills I can take you there." Kurt said

I guess that wasn't the first time Kurt had gone to that breakfast place. I wondered how long he had been driving around Steele?

"Thank you very much" I said

"You're welcome" Kurt said

I heard my work phone go off, it was the email from Steele

Brie, Basil and Bacon Omelet, fruit cup and a Matcha to drink. Order whatever you like.

-Steele Everest

CEO

Everest Corp

Email: steeleeverest@everestcorp.com

Phone Number: 1-858-345-1633

I quickly sent Steele an email back.

Thank you very much, I will be back as soon as I can.-Skylan Mills

I needed to add a signature too. It looked unprofessional to not have one. It should have been the first feature I did to my email.

We arrived at the restaurant. That place looked extremely nice and expensive. I glanced at the menu for a moment. You have to be kidding me. This place was too much for one person. I didn't even know what to order or if I should order anything. Maybe we needed to go to McDonald's for me. I didn't want Steele to spend that much money on me. He had already done more than enough. I told the lady what Steele wanted and asked for it to-go. It was done pretty quickly.

We arrived back at Everest Corp. I had decided I wasn't going to eat today. I jetted to the elevator to try to go back up to the 25 floor so I wouldn't run into Bridgett. That girl was a snake. Plus I have to make 12,000 copies of these invitations. I didn't have time to argue with her.

I knocked on Steele's door.

Steele was at his desk, typing away. He didn't even look away.

"Come in" Steele said

"I have all your food." I said

"Thank you, I sent that email to you to make those 12,000 copies. I need all those in envelopes please. The envelopes should be at your desk. I need them done by tomorrow morning at 10 A.M." Steele said when a professional mellow voice.

"Okay, I will have that done. Thank you. Is there anything else I can help you with?" I said

YOU FREAKING KIDDING ME? THAT HAD TO BE A JOKE. ON THE OUTSIDE I WAS CHILL ON THE INSIDE I DON'T THINK I COULD FREAK OUT ENOUGH. THAT IS 24

HOURS!

"No thank you. I just really need those letters done by tomorrow. After you have them done, I would like it if you would give them to Bridgett." Steele said

"Okay, I can do that" I said

I NEEDED HELP DOING THAT! HOW IN THE WORLD DOES SOMEONE DO THAT? I WAS GOING TO BE THERE ALL NIGHT LONG.

I went back to my office and had a panic attack. That was fun. I wasn't sure about anyone else but the panic attacks I experienced weren't healthy or fun. I sat at my desk to look at my computer. I needed to look for that email. I found it, I was impressed when I figured out it was a charity for a church. It fit him perfectly. He did go to church every Wednesday and Sunday. That made sense that he would do charity for a church. When did he find time to arrange a charity?

I had a fancy printer/fax machine in my office. I was happy I didn't have to walk far to print the invitations to the charity event. I hoped the printer wouldn't break. I only printed 100 then I started putting them in the envelopes. I put it on elegant paper so it was sumptuous. It was simple so I didn't want to make it on plain paper. Instead of licking them, I found a stamp that had his logo on it and pressed that stamp on every single one of them.

I was going to be there all night. Also I knew my hands would hurt the next day.

I turned on some music in my office. I decided to call my Grandma Maggie to inform her what was going on at work.

"Hey grandma, I am going to be here all night. I have work that needs to be done by 10AM tomorrow and it's a bunch. I don't know when I will be done but I will call you when I am done." I said

"What do you have to do that is going to make you so late?" Grandma Maggie asked

"I am putting invitations in envelopes and they need to be done by tomorrow morning." I said

"At least you will make up for the time you missed yesterday. Call me when you are done" Grandma Maggie said

I worked on the invitations all day long. Steele didn't give me anything else to do. I guess these invitations were important. I looked at the clock, it was about 1PM. Steele walked into my office

"Kurt is going for a lunch run. Do you want anything?" Steele said

"Isn't that my job?" I said

"Usually, I would send you but I have you on something very important. I am just going to send him. It won't be the last time I send Mr. Busch. Sometimes we are so busy that it's better for him to go grab our food." Steele said

"Okay, I will take anything. It doesn't matter what you order me." I said

"Alright, he will be back soon." Steele said

"Thanks" I said

"You are getting those done quickly. How many have you done?" Steele said

"I think I have only done maybe eighteen hundred, I am sorry but I don't think I will finish all these. I am going to try." I said

"I will come see how much you have done at 5 PM" Steele said

"Alright, I am looking forward to that food" I said while laughing.

"Me too, see you later Miss Mills" Steele said

"See you later, Mr. Everest" I said

Steele probably thought I was weird sitting on the floor doing all those invitations. Some projects were better done on the floor because I had more space. I would be there all night so I figured that I might as well sit where I want.

Sometime during the day Kurt came in and sat my food on my desk. I didn't even see him come into my office. I just happened to look up at my desk and saw it. I guess I was so into that project I wasn't aware that someone came into my office. I looked at the clock, it was 3 PM. I had finished about three thousand invitations. I decided to take a thirty minute break to eat lunch. The food Kurt brought me was delightful. I didn't know where it was from but it was incredible. It had to be a different cultural meal. I knew that it was expensive. How was he still wealthy? He spends more than anyone should on food!

I started back on the invitations. Steele said he would check on me at about 5 o'clock in the evening. He walked in about 5:30 PM.

"Miss Mills, I am sorry. I realize I said I would check on you at 5 o'clock in the evening but I wasn't paying attention to the clock and was in a business meeting. I realize it's 5:30 in the evening. How are you doing?" Steele said

"I am doing good. Sorry I have zoned out. I didn't realize it was already 5:30 in the evening, I am really trying to finish these invitations." I said

"How many have you done?" Steele said

"I probably have done about forty two hundred." I said

"I have some work left to do but I will be back around 7. Are you still going to be here?" Steele said

"Of course I will still be here." I said

"Do you want dinner? I figure you might be here all night" Steele said

"Yes please, I don't care what you order" I said

"Alright, dinner will be here for you at 7 o'clock" Steele said

"Thanks" I said

His cell phone started to ring.

"Hello, Steele Everest" Steele answered the phone.

He waved good-bye as he walked out the door

I resumed the invitations. I definitely didn't think I would finish the invitations in time. Why did he give me such a big project at the last minute?

I had seeped into the project so much that I needed some fresh air. I guess about 6:30 in the evening, I started to feel a headache coming on with all those invitations. I walked outside to inhale some fresh air. Everyone at the office had already left. It was close to dark outside and the air felt fresh, the breeze had a little chill to it. I had been stuck inside all day, the outside air felt much better than the stuffy air inside. I sat on the bench outside, I saw it the other day when my grandma came to pick me up but I didn't read it. It said In Memory of Michael, Brandi, and Mac. I wondered who those people were. I wondered if I should ask Steele.

The bench made me think about the sitting area the school gave my parents after they died. My mother was a kindergarten teacher and my dad was the principal. They were both employees at the school for a long time before they died. Their names were Michael and Brandi. Even though everyone called my dad Mike instead of Michael.

I saw Steele coming from the sidewalk carrying a bag of food. I wasn't expecting to run into him when I came down here.

"Do you want some help Mr. Everest?" I asked

"No thank you. I have it. What are you doing down here?" Steele asked

"I needed some fresh air. I thought you weren't coming to my office till 7?" I asked

"I became hungry a little sooner than expected" Steele said

"I am not really hungry. I don't usually eat a lot." I said

"Why not? I love food! I can never consume enough. I try to eat healthy. Every once in a while I will step outside the health train and eat junk food." Steele said as he laughed.

"I don't know. I just don't have an appetite." I said

"We might have to fix that...I am joking" Steele said with a cute laugh.

We rode up the elevator together. As much as I wanted to fantasize about kissing him in the elevator, nothing happened. He walked me to my office. I still wondered why Steele was single for so long.

"How many invitations have you done?" Steele asked

"I think I have about forty-eight hundred" I said

"I have some papers I need to have done tonight. It will take me about an hour. Do you want me to help?" Steele asked

I almost accepted his help but I wanted to show him I could do it. I was close to half way done. For a brief moment, I wondered if it was a trick. It could have very well been a test.

"No, I think I have it. I am about halfway done." I said

As much as I would have loved to spend time with my incredible boss, I needed to prove to him that I could complete all of the invitations.

"Alright, if you need help just call me. I can come help. Goodnight." Steele said

"Thank you for offering to help and thank you for the food" I said

Steele nodded his head up and down and walked out.

I resumed my work so that way I could finish the invitations. I knew I would be done around 5 in the morning.

Time went by quick, the next I knew it was about 3 in the morning. I was about to fall asleep. I had about 10,200 done at that time. I couldn't believe I was almost done. I had done around 10,200 invitations. I was mentally and physically exhausted. I could barely move. For the first time in a while I was actually hungry. I looked at my phone right quick. I had multiple missed calls from Steele and my Grandma Maggie.

I decided to text both of them since it was 3 in the morning.

First I texted my Grandma Maggie, I told her I was still working to call me around 6. I texted Steele, I told him I was at 10,200 and I should be done by 5 in the morning.

He immediately called me.

"Hello" I said

"Hello, Skylan I saw you are at 10,200. Have you taken a break since I last saw you?" Steele asked

"I wanted to have these invitations done before 10 o'clock in the morning. I am about to make some coffee and walk downstairs." I said

"I am going to bring you coffee and breakfast since you haven't finished or took a break since last night" Steele said

"Thank you, I don't even know what is open right now in Austin" I said

"Do you care what I order you?" Steele asked

"Absolutely not" I said

"Ok, I will be there shortly. Oh how do you like your coffee?" Steele

said

"Sugar and milk" I said

"Alright, goodbye" Steele said

"Bye" I said in a polite way as I was still doing the invitations

I only had 1,800 left to go and I did it all on my own. I didn't think I could've been so tired in my life!

I walked outside to breathe in some fresh air. I breathed the fresh air in so deeply that I felt it in my lungs. I did a few more to wake me up. I had grabbed some water before I left so I decided to drink some water while I was down there. I sat outside for about 15 minutes.

15

FIFTEEN minutes later…

On the way back to my office, I heard my phone start ringing. It was Steele.

"Hello" I said

"Are you still awake?" Steele asked as he giggled.

"Yes, I just walked into my office from outside" I said with a smile on my face.

"Great, I'm about to head that way. I should be there in about 20 minutes. I cooked you an omelet and made you some coffee. I hope that is okay. I knew the coffee stand was closed. Most places don't open till 6 or 7 am. I need to buy a coffee maker for you tomorrow." Steele said

"Yes, that is fine. Thank you for everything" I said

I decided to do a few more while Steele was on his way to the office. I turned on some music, and about 30 minutes later, I looked up. Steele was leaning up against the door frame.

"Hello, I didn't want to interrupt you. I haven't been here long. I'm surprised you didn't hear me come in. I love the dance moves you are doing." Steele said with a smile.

"I zoned out. I'm trying to finish these invitations by 5 in the morning." I said

"Why 5? I told you they didn't have to be turned in until 10 am." Steele said

"I set a deadline for myself" I said

"Keep up the good work. I will be back around 7 or 8." Steele said as he grinned.

"Okay. I might be here. I'm not sure." I said

"Okay, that's fine as long as you are here at 10 to turn those in" Steele said

"I will be in my office" I said

I hope I am here at 10 am. I'm past tired now. We fixated on each other again for a moment.

"Oh. Let me take that food from you. Thank you for the food by the way" I said

"Here you go, you're welcome. Good luck on the rest of those" Steele said

I walked to my desk, sat down and ate. It tasted so good, I never had anything so good. I wasn't sure if it was because I was hungry or he was that good of a cook.

It took about 10 minutes to eat.

I zoned back into the invitations and the next thing I knew, I was done. 12,000 invitations done. I looked at the clock, 5:16 AM. I did it. I had a couch in my office. It was very comfortable and honestly I wasn't sure why I had it in there but I set an alarm for 8. I heard my alarm go off.

I woke up and there was a blanket on me. A note saying *Congratulations you did it! I'm proud of you! Thank you very much! -Steele Everest*

That made me extremely proud. Bridgett was about to come up. I was so excited to see Bridgett because I was ready to turn in all those invitations at 8 am. I never thought I would be excited to see Bridgett. 12,000 invitations were done!

"Hello, Bridgett, I have something for you. 12,000 invitations! Before 10AM." I said

She usually came up here around 8:15AM. I figured I would just give them to her now instead of at 10 AM. I was already done with them.

"Why are you so happy?" Bridgett said

"I did all those in less than 24 hours. I didn't think I would finish them!" I said

"Okay, you need to quit being so happy. This was all a test. This happens to every assistant" Bridgett said

"I don't care. I am proud of myself!" I said

Bridgett didn't know anything about me. She didn't know that I struggled with depression or that I didn't think I could do it. I stayed awake without falling asleep. She didn't know that those invitations were the first accomplishment I had done since I had graduated from college.

I heard the deep sexy voice behind me.

"Thank you Bridgett" Steele Everest said

"You're welcome Mr. Everest" Bridgett said

"Do you want breakfast, Skylan?" Steele asked

"I absolutely do!" I said with a smile on my face.

"Good. What do you want?" Steele asked

"Snooze, an A.M. Eatery" I said

"Alright. Call in our order. I will have Kurt pick it up." Steele said

"Okay! Thank you!" I said

"Are you always this hyper when you first wake up?" Steele asked

"Absolutely NOT!" I said

"Okay" Steele laughed

"Do you need anything?" I asked

"If you don't mind, I would like my schedule for tomorrow made up" Steele said

"Will do! Anything else?" I asked

"Yes, I wanted to tell you good job on doing those invitations all on your own" Steele said

I had never been so excited in my life. Only because I worked all night!

"Thank you" I said

I went to make his schedule for tomorrow. It usually took me about 2 hours because he did so much during the day. I was glad I slept for at least a few hours. I was determined to make it through that day. I was afraid that I could have passed out standing up. I decided to go downstairs to grab an energy drink. While I walked down there I decided to call my Grandma Maggie.

"I finished all the invitations" I said with excitement.

I didn't even let her say hello or anything

"Congratulations. Are you coming home?" Grandma Maggie said

"I'm sorry. I have a couch in my office so I just slept on it. I just went to sleep because I was so tired. I honestly don't think I could have stayed awake long enough until you arrived." I said

"Are you going to come home and take a shower?" Grandma Maggie said

"I don't think I can" I said

"I am sure Mr. Everest would let you if you asked" Grandma Maggie said

I saw Kurt walk into the building, he came straight to me.

"You are probably right but I feel like if I go home then I will fall asleep and sleep till tomorrow. I have to go grandma, my food is here." I said

I have never been so happy to see pancakes!

"Would you like me to take mine out of your hands?" I said

"No, Miss Mills. I have it! I heard you had a late night so I can take it to your office." Kurt said

"Okay thank you." I said

I grabbed my drink from the vending machine

"It's my pleasure." Kurt said

We headed to the elevator, the ride up was quiet. We went all the way to the 25th floor by ourselves. I could have asked him questions because he was Mr. Everest driver. He probably knew everything about him. I just couldn't work up the nerve to ask him about anything.

We stepped out of the elevator, and we both went straight to my office.

"Enjoy" Kurt said

"Thanks, Kurt" I said

"You're welcome Miss Mills" Kurt said

While I did the invitations I thought that I was as tired as I could've ever been but nope. I was more tired the next day, I honestly didn't know how I had made it that far. I started to eat my food, oh my why did I pick that. I should have asked for something else, what if he didn't like it. I should have picked a place that he had told me to go to before. Halfway done with my food, Steele walked in.

"How is your breakfast?" Steele said

I tried to hurry and finish my bite because I didn't like talking with my mouth full.

"It's really good! You could have picked the place for breakfast" I said

"Thanks. I used to try new places all the time because I enjoy food. I don't try new places as much as I used to because I am so busy with work." Steele said

"I have never really been into food. It's not my thing." I said

"Oh really, not your thing. So what is your thing?" Steele asked

Seriously, I didn't know that answer.

"I don't know anymore. Ever since high school, life has been downhill. I don't really have a thing I guess anymore." I said

I wondered why Steele was so easy to talk to. That might have been the reason he was a good businessman.

"I can tell you are a hard worker. You like working alone more than with a group. Are you an introvert? If you don't mind me asking." Steele asked

"Thanks. I used to be an extrovert. The past few years I have changed. May I ask who Michael, Brandi and Mac are?" I asked

Steele scratched his head

"Umm, Mac was one of the original founders of this company. I will have to tell you about Michael and Brandi a different time" Steele said with hesitation

"So why is it called Everest Corporation?" I asked

"He died before it became a company. When he died we were only talking about it. We were going to name it something else but before he died he told me that he wanted me to name it Everest Corporation. It was one of our last conversations we had." Steele said

"I am sorry. Thanks for telling me." I said

"It was a hard time. I threw myself into the company after he died. I knew I had to make it successful. I guess I kind of lost my social life in the process. He was my best friend and my brother. I haven't talked about him to an employee before." Steele said

"May I ask how he died?" I asked with hesitation

I was young when my parents died. I couldn't imagine how he felt. His brother who was also his best friend, DIED. How do you deal with that?

"Maybe another time" Steele said with a loose smile.

Steele slowly started walking away

"Hey, thanks for telling me the little information you did tell me" I said with a soft, kind voice.

"Yeah, I am going to head back to my office. Are you good?" Steele said shortly after he tripped over his own feet.

"Yes, sir" I said as I drifted off into my head.

After I listened to all that, I had another flashback about my parents

It was about a month after they were killed. I didn't want to go to the cemetery but my Grandma Maggie made me go. I wanted to stay away because I didn't want their death to be real. Even though I knew it was real, it would be more real if I saw their grave. I just wanted their death to feel like they were on vacation or were on a business trip but they were still coming back.

I was surprised that Steele hadn't talked to at least one employee about his brother. I wondered if no one had asked about it or if he just hadn't told anyone? Maybe he was just lying to me. I wasn't sure. I didn't need to think too much about it.

After I was done with his schedule, I saw that he had sent me an email. One of the many business involvements he was part of in the food industry. I was surprised he didn't weigh 300 pounds. I hadn't looked up all the restaurants he owned or was associated with. He mostly had meetings all day long. Each meeting was with different branches of his company but one day a week of each month he would go to all of the businesses that he owned. I bet that was the best part of running all of his businesses.

I went back to thinking about his brother, I wished I knew the whole story about his brother, Mac Everest. He died so young. I tried to look him up but all I could find was a son, brother and friend that died too young. It was like someone covered everything up from what happened. There was nothing about him. It was almost like he didn't exist. Steele was this huge billionaire, however I could barely find anything on the web about his brother. I thought that was kind of odd. I looked up Steele Everest, and many topics came up. I decided to take another route. I looked up his criminal record. Nothing. I wasn't going to worry about it at that moment, I just knew there was more to the story. I was going to figure it out too.

Finally, the day for me was almost over. I made the schedule for all the places next week. The schedule for the next day was updated. I had called everyone to confirm their meeting. I wondered if he wore suits to all his businesses.

I guess it depended on what type of business he was dealing with that day.

It was 3:44PM. I was done with everything Steele had asked me to do. I was ready to return home. I was wearing the same clothes as I wore the day before and it was finally Friday! The week had been a whole new level of busy and a whole new level of tired.

I couldn't get the thought out of my head about why he hired me for this job?

I had about an hour left of work to go. If I didn't fall asleep first.

My work phone started to ring. It was Steele.

"Miss Mills, can you come to my office please?" Steele said with a straightforward voice.

"Yes sir I can. I will be there right away" I said with a sharp and pleasant voice.

"You can go home, but I wanted to ask you. I know you have been here all night. Would you like to come to church on Sunday? I don't want to force you but I wanted to see if you might want to come." Steele asked while rubbing his hand on the back of his neck.

"Umm I don't really know how to respond to that? I haven't been to church since my parents died" I said as my face turned a cherry red.

"You don't have to, I just thought I would ask." Steele said

"Okay, thanks. Maybe another Sunday, I was really going to try to rest this weekend. Also I don't have a car so I will have to request an Uber to come pick me up so I might be here a little longer." I said

"No need to request an Uber. I will be here for another 3 hours or so. Kurt can take you home. He is waiting downstairs" Steele said

"Thank you very much. I am very thankful for your generosity. You have been so nice to me since I started working here" I said

That guy was too nice for anyone. Why was he still single? Other than the fact that he worked harder than a beat dog. I wished I knew more about that guy.

I went back to my office. Grabbed my purse and headed downstairs. I was ready to jump in bed. My bed was calling my name! I couldn't leave that building fast enough.

After Kurt dropped me off, I went straight to my room and went to sleep. Honestly, hygiene wasn't the top of my priority. Sleeping was on the top of that list. I didn't care about anyone else or anything else. I was going to sleep.

16

twenty-four hours and **SIXTEEN** minutes later...

I woke up Saturday night. I couldn't believe I slept for over twenty-four hours. I would say that would be a record time for me. I didn't know if my grandma yelled at me or not. I was in such deep sleep I could have slept through an earthquake, tornado or fire.

When I woke up, I kind of thought about the question Steele asked me. Would you like to come to church on Sunday? I haven't had someone ask me to go to church in years. I didn't want to say anything to anyone, especially my grandma. I knew she would have said we needed to go. I was just too tired to do anything. I would rather lay in bed all day. Unfortunately, I need to hop out of bed then go take a shower. I just didn't want to do it right away.

I watched television most of the day Sunday and slept the rest. I decided to be lazy that whole weekend. It was about 7 o'clock at night, so I decided I needed to jump in the shower. It was time since the last time I took a shower was Thursday morning. I slowly forced myself to crawl out of bed. I took my time as I walked to the bathroom. I decided to take a bath instead of a shower. I turned the water on at a perfect temperature. I poured some essential oil bath soap in it. I went to my sink, I washed my face with my vanity brush then put on a face mask. Walked to the bathtub and turned the water off. Then hopped in the bathtub. It was a pleasurable temperature. I turned on the jets, I figured I needed it. I sat there and thought about good memories. I tried to relax since I had a whole week of work to do. I laid in there for about 10 minutes then fell asleep. I woke up to look at the clock, I was in there for about an hour. I turned off the jets then pulled the plug from the drain.

I stood up to turn the shower on. I could never take a bath without taking a shower directly after. Since I had sat in there for over an hour the hot water had become cold. It felt extremely refreshing to take a shower. I stood there for a moment while I felt the hot water hit my head then go down my entire body. I washed the face mask off of my face that I had put on before the bath. After I took the mask off I felt my face, it felt rejuvenated.

I picked up my shampoo, I squirted a small amount of it onto my palm. I massaged the shampoo into my hair until it lathered. I went back under the showerhead, as I stood there the soap in my hair washed out of my hair and into the drain. I grabbed the conditioner then put a small amount of it in my palm, I put the conditioner throughout my hair, as I let it run through my fingers. I stepped under the showerhead once again to rinse out the conditioner. Shortly after I washed and rinsed my body with coconut body wash. The water started to lose its heat. I stepped out of the shower, then grabbed the towel. I walked to my closet, I picked out a ZZ Top shirt and some underwear. I went straight back to my bed. My head hit the pillow, soon after I was asleep.

When I woke up, I heard my alarm go off. I kept my eyes closed as I thought to myself, I was ready for the weekend. I opened my eyes, I completely comprehended it was only Monday. Tomorrow I had a therapy appointment with Teresa, I was definitely not ready to go to that appointment. I was delighted I had another day to prepare myself for therapy. I didn't like opening up in therapy. I didn't see there being a day where I would open up in therapy.

I forced myself to roll out of bed even though I still rolled out of bed late. I wasn't able to enjoy the shower like I usually would in the mornings. I was grateful I took one the time before. I pushed myself to put make-up on and dress nice. Everything I did was mentally and physically difficult. I wished I would've enjoyed activities like everyone else but I didn't have the energy to do anything. I hardly had energy to go to work. It took all the energy I did have to make it through a full day of work. If I didn't have to go to work and therapy, I might have been more excited about life. Honestly that wasn't true. Before I had that job and before I started therapy I wasn't excited about life at all. I was just tired all the time. I didn't want to do anything.

It slipped my mind that I needed a stupid car. I walked downstairs to talk to my Grandma Maggie.

"Hey, I need a car for work. When are we going to pick up a rental? I am sick of people driving me around or waiting on people." I said

"Call your boss. Inform him that you are going to rent a rental. Then ask him if it's alright if you are late? I guess we will go get a rental this morning if it's okay with Steele." Grandma Maggie said

"YES, I will call right now. I need a car. I can't take this any longer" I said as I jumped up and down with excitement.

"Okay, I will be in the car. I need to call my work as well." Grandma Maggie said

"Okay, I will be out there as soon as I'm off the phone with Steele." I said

I was almost ready but I was ready to have a car more. I was over and done with being driven around by other people that I was willing to do anything at that point.

 I decided not to put makeup on. I packed it in my makeup bag so that way I could put it on in the car.

"Hello, this is Steele Everest" Steele said

"Hello, this is Skylan Mills. I am going to be late today because I am going to pick up a rental since I still don't have a car." I said

"Okay that is fine. Can you grab breakfast on your way?" Steele asked

"What would you like?" I asked

"Anything healthy, just surprise me" Steele said

I rolled my eyes because that guy was not limited when it came to food

"Okay, see you in a little bit" I said

I decided since I was going to be late that I would just put a little bit of makeup on at the house.

Finally, I was off the phone. I headed back up the stairs to finish getting ready. Put some powder on my face and put some mascara on my eyelashes. I grab my purse and head out the door. I was ready to have a car again. I couldn't fathom being driven around all day any longer. I never understood why Steele wanted to be driven around all day.

We had to drive into Austin to rent a car so that meant a long drive, which meant the loud voices were about to begin.

"Don't wreck this car. It's a rental. Which means that it has to be returned. Can you do that?" Grandma Maggie said

"Of course you would say that. The wreck wasn't even my fault, it was someone else's fault. It's not my fault that no one in the world knows how to drive but me. Maybe I am meant to die the same way my parents did." I said

"Don't you dare say that ever again! You are not meant to die the same way they did" Grandma Maggie yelled at me.

"How do you know? I was in a wreck and it wasn't my fault." I said

"You didn't die, did you?" Grandma Maggie said

"Have you ever thought about what happened to that family?" Grandma Maggie said

"No, those people took my parents away from me. There is so much I missed out on because my parents died when I was younger because of a stupid drunk driver" I said

"Maybe we should take Steele up on his offer to go to church. I think it's time to start going to church again." Grandma Maggie said

"If I say yes will you shut up? I am sick of this car ride already." I said

Secretly I did want to go but at the same time I really wanted to say no because she asked

"This Sunday we will go. It's been too long since we both went to church" Grandma Maggie said

"Yes, did you forget why I quit going or did you forget what happened?" I said

"I could never forget the accident that my son was in and I know that was the last time you were in a church" Grandma Maggie said

"Really, you act like it didn't happen. You haven't talked about it since the day of the funeral" I said

"You have no clue what I have gone through since all of this happened. I have taken care of you, may I add that you haven't made it easy lately." Grandma Maggie said

"Take care of me, are you serious, I don't do anything. I try really hard not to talk to you or bother you at all!" I said

"I pay the bills like the water bill you run up when you take long showers or leave the water running when you brush your teeth. I pay the electricity bills that you run up because you never turn off the TV. You might stay in your room all day but you don't pay bills. All you want to do is fight with me." Grandma Maggie said

We finally arrived at the rental place. I assumed my Grandma Maggie took care of everything because I knew nothing about car rentals. I was sure she has dealt with rental problems multiple times in her long life that she had lived.

"Whatever, you just want to fight with me." I said

I stepped out of the car. I slammed the door so hard I was surprised it didn't fall off.

I walked into the rental building. Immediately, as soon as I walked in, it smelled like old women. The best way I knew how to explain it was if a person had ever been in a nursing home was what the rental place smelled like. Some positive words I could say about my grandma's house was that it didn't smell like an old lady.

My grandma walked in right behind me. She walked up to the front desk and immediately started talking to the lady.

"Hello, my name is Maggie Mills. This is my granddaughter Skylan Mills. I called earlier for a car rental."

My Grandma Maggie's customer service voice and personal voice amazed me with the change she made of them. She would completely change into another person.

"One moment, I will go pull the car up to the door" the front desk lady said

"Thank you very much" Grandma Maggie said

I just stood there, tongue tied. I had nothing to say, Grandma Maggie had done everything. My face probably looked like I was bored with the world. I was ready to drive my rental car to grab breakfast. The woman from the front desk walked in the door.

"Here are the keys ma'am" the front desk lady said

She handed the keys to my Grandma Maggie.

Immediately, Grandma Maggie reached out like she was going to hand the keys to me then pulled the keys back quickly.

"Don't wreck this car" Grandma Maggie said

I rolled my eyes and she finally gave me the keys

"I won't" I said

I walked outside to hop in the car. It wasn't the most stylish car in the world. It was a 2020 Chevy Spark. The exterior was a summit white. The interior was black with leather seats. It had heated seats in the front so that was a plus. It had a fold down armrest that was rather comfortable. The front seat was extremely roomy but the backseat looked like you could barely fit a baby in it. Not that it really mattered. I didn't have any friends who would ride with me nor did I have a baby. The car had a screen right above the air vents. Under the screen were the air vents, under them were the controls to the air vents; the speed of the vents and the position of them. I wish the rental company would have given me a nicer car.

As soon as I sat in the car I turned the music on. Christian music was the first station that came on. It made me think again about going to church with Steele and my Grandma Maggie. It had been so long since I had been in a church. Would it still be the same? What would I wear to church? When I was little I knew how to wear dresses but do people still wear dresses to church? Many different questions started flowing through my mind about church. Maybe after all the years that I had stayed out of church it was time to go back. I chose to think of another topic in my head.

Since I was going to do it soon, I decided to hook my phone up to the rental. I looked up healthy food places. I had almost forgotten that I needed to pick up food for Steele. Heck there I was thinking about Steele and church. How did I almost forget that I needed to pick up food for him?

I finally found a food place called the Picnik. More than likely he had already eaten there. All he said was something healthy. I typed the directions to the Picnik into my phone. It was approximately 45 minutes away. The main reason being because of traffic congestion. There was always so much traffic in Austin.

I pulled up to the restaurant, parked my car. I immediately noticed there were a bunch of people in there. I was able to make my order after waiting for a little bit.

I ordered Steele, an Avocado Toast on gluten-free bread with basil pesto, smashed avocado, tomato, and poached egg with chili flake hemp seeds.

It sounded so good I decided to order two of them. I hurried to receive my order then headed to the office. I felt like I was extremely late. I was mentally preparing myself that Steele was going to yell at me or worse, fire me. It started to become an expectation I had of myself and Steele every morning I went into the office.

I pulled into the parking garage. There was a man in clothes dressed like he had been homeless for years. Since Kurt was a bodyguard and usually near the parking garage I decided to give him a call. I didn't want to jump out of the car since he looked so scary.

17

SEVENTEEN strangers

"Kurt, this is Skylan. There is a guy who is standing in front of my car and isn't leaving. Can you come over to my car please?" I asked scared but kindly.

"Yes Miss Mills, I will be there shortly." Kurt said in a professional manner.

Kurt drove over there very quickly. It happened so fast, Kurt put the guy on the ground then put the homeless man in handcuffs then called the police. It was strange, I had never seen that guy in my life.

I was in such shock that when I finally caught my breath I was in the police station with Kurt, Steele and my Grandma Maggie. I was also surrounded by a bunch of police officers. I still don't remember how I made it from the parking garage to the police station.

"...can you describe the man for us ma'am?" Police officer said

"All I could remember was a man standing in front of my car. He looked homeless or lost" I said

I honestly couldn't remember much. It all happened so fast.

"What time is it?" I asked

"It's noon" Steele said

I felt so bad because that shouldn't have happened. I didn't even know if Steele received his food.

"Did you get your food?" I asked Steele unhinged.

"Don't worry about that" Steele said

I felt so bad about all of it. Everyone in the parking lot that day, it just had to be me. I didn't understand why some strange guy would walk up to my car.

At that point I just wanted to go home. I didn't want to go to work or anywhere but home.

"Miss Mills, I think you should go home. You can come to work tomorrow." Steele said

"Thank you. It's like you read my mind" I said

"Alright, officer, are you done?" Grandma Maggie said

"Yes, we are done. If we have any more questions, someone will contact you" the officer said

For many years, I couldn't imagine going through what I had gone through. I didn't know why it happened to me. Why me? Anything that could go bad always happened to me. I was past being ready to leave the police station. As I sat in that police station it had brought me back to the night my parents died. I felt so alone. I didn't know what to do as a child. I was young and afraid of what would come next. The one piece of information I knew for a fact was the last time I was in a police station was when I found out my parents were never coming back.

While being an adult, sitting in the police station, the only thing I knew then was I didn't think I would be able to go to a car without searching for someone in it or around it. Maybe I needed to start riding a bus. Cars were becoming too much for me. I wondered what would happen next on the car incident list.

The car ride home was a blur. I don't remember any of it other than the fact that I knew My Grandma Maggie drove us home. When we arrived home I went straight to my room and slept until the next day.

18

EIGHTEEN hours later...

When I woke up that morning all I wanted was for the past 24 hours to be a nightmare that I could wake up from. Nothing was going to change that. I did my usual morning routine, stumbled in the shower. Since I did all my thinking in the shower, I didn't want to stay in there long. Every time I closed my eyes the whole car incident happened again. I hurried up and jumped out of the shower. It might have been the quickest shower I ever took. I brushed my teeth, then went straight to my closet. I picked out some clothes for work. I sat down at my vanity to put my makeup on. Shortly after sitting there, while looking in the mirror. I thought to myself, what is wrong with me? I started to think of all the bad thoughts I always had in my head. I started to put my foundation on and the more makeup I put on, the more confident I felt. If only I could change the inside of me. I headed downstairs, and my grandma had some food fixed. I wasn't hungry but I decided I should eat. Nothing was really said when I first walked downstairs. She looked at me and I looked at her.

The silence broke when my phone started to ring, I immediately searched for it in my purse. I pulled it out, when I read who was calling I answered immediately.

"Hello, how can I help you?" I said with a professional tone.

"Good morning, I sent Mr. Busch for you today. I figured that you wouldn't want to ride in your car after what happened. If you don't feel like coming in today that is fine too. I completely understand."

Steele said with remorse.

"Yes, I want to come in. Thank you for sending him, I think I will take you up on that offer. I will be in soon. Do you need anything before I come into the office?" I said

"No, thank you. I am glad you decided to come in today. I will see you soon" Steele said in a cheerful tone.

Are you kidding me? Who wouldn't want to come into work? Just seeing you makes my day!

"Headed to work Grandma Maggie, I might call you to come pick me up from work" I said, happier than before I talked on the phone with Steele.

"Okay, I will have my phone on me" Grandma Maggie said with remorse.

I enjoyed everyone being nice but I also didn't want pity because of what had happened to me.

When I walked outside, Kurt was already waiting for me. When I hopped to the car door, Kurt opened the door for me. I climbed in the back seat, I sat in the seat closest to the door. I hated sitting in the middle, I never had a perfect reason for sitting on the outside than preferred to the middle. I thought out of respect I would put my seatbelt on for Kurt and Steele. I sat back there quietly without saying one word. Kurt put some country music on so it wasn't complete silence in the car. When we arrived in the city, Kurt reminded me of my job. It wasn't that I was thinking about anything specific but I just stared out the window the whole ride.

"Miss Mills, do you want me to stop at a restaurant to grab breakfast?" Kurt asked

"Yes, absolutely. Do you have a place in mind?" I asked

"Yes, I do. We are about to come up on it." Kurt said

Thankfully I had Kurt that morning. I was completely out of my mind. I knew I needed to go to work. I wasn't sure why that day I needed it compared to all the other days that I didn't want to go to work.

"Would you like to order it on your phone?" Kurt asked

"Yes, what is the place called?" I asked

"Ma'am it is called The Omelettry" Kurt said

"Okay thank you, I will order. Is there anything you would like to order?" I said

"No thank you ma'am I already ate this morning but thank you for asking." Kurt said

I pulled my phone out, I looked it up. I ordered 2 Popeye's Favorite at La Carte. It had Fresh Spinach, crisp bacon and sautéed onions inside a cheese omelet topped with sour cream. There were healthier choices on the menu but I didn't have the time to look through the whole menu. I just knew that what I ordered sounded good. I expected that Steele would enjoy it. I was satisfied with myself a little that morning because I wasn't too late to work. It did help that Kurt was there to pick me up.

"We are here at the restaurant" Kurt said

"Thank you, I can let myself out. I might need you to open the door so I can put the food in the car when I arrive back" I said

I stepped out of the vehicle then went into the building. The building was mostly basic but I knew it had to be good if Kurt was recommending it. I was greeted immediately when I walked in the restaurant.

"How can I help you?" a worker asked

"I ordered a to go order online" I said

"What is the name on the order" the worker asked

"Skylan Mills" I said with a forced smile

"Ok, here it is right here. That will be $23.55" the worker said

I pulled out the credit card that Steele had given me for all the expenses. The worker swiped the card then gave it right back. The worker handed me two receipts, one for me to sign and one to keep. I signed one, then gave it back. I grabbed the food then walked out. Right when I was about to walk out the door, Kurt had the door open.

"Thank you Kurt" I said

"You're welcome. Let me take some of that out of your hands" Kurt said

"Ok thank you" I said

I handed him some of the food. When we arrived at the car, he opened the door. I sat the food inside the car then jumped in.

"Thank you, Kurt" I said

"You're welcome" Kurt said

Once we started on the way to work, not much was said.

"Miss Mills, we are here at the office. Hold on one moment and let me open the door" Kurt said professionally.

"Okay" I said

"Here you go Miss Mills, I hope you have a great day" Kurt said nice and professional.

"Thank you, have a great day" I said nicely.

I walked through the door. I skipped talking to anyone and went straight to the elevator. I walked into my office, there was a note from Steele. It said I'm sorry for what happened yesterday.

I didn't know why Steele was saying sorry. He didn't do anything. I grabbed a pen and a piece of paper. I walked to his office, knocked on the door.

"Come in" Steele said

I walked in expecting him to tell me a list of arrangements I needed to do that day but that wasn't what came out.

"How are you today?" Steele asked kindly.

"I am still a little shaken up from yesterday but I'm here to work." I said with confidence.

"Great, today I need you to be in here to take notes while I am in the meeting today, can you do that?" Steele said

"Absolutely sir, is that all?" I asked

"That is all I have for you right now, be back here in about 30 minutes to start getting ready" Steele said very professionally.

"Okay" I said with a smile.

"You are excused. Thank you" Steele said

"You're welcome" I said

As I started to walk out the door, I turned back around while I looked at Steele.

"May I ask you why you left an apology note?" I asked kindly

"Let's talk about that after we are done with all the meetings today" Steele said

"Okay thank you" I said

I walked out the door, back to my office. I sat down and thought about what the letter could mean. He didn't do anything for him to say he was sorry. During what happened the day before and the note he had left on my desk I couldn't think about anything else. I really hoped it wouldn't affect my day. I tried to update his schedule. Shortly after I was done, I went to Steele's office.

I knocked on his door

"Come in" Steele said loudly

"Hello Steele" I said

"Do you have a pen and paper?" Steele asked

"Yes I do" I said

"Okay, I need you to write down each company meeting, the person I am in a meeting with and anything else you think might be important. Can you do that?" Steele said

"Yes I can" I said with confidence.

Even though I was scared as all get out, I wanted to sound confident to him

I went all day to the meetings. It was almost like I was writing everything down but I was in a blur all day long. The same things kept going through my head. Why did we need to talk after the meetings? Why couldn't we talk then? Why did that homeless man pick me to ruin my life? Those three questions kept going through my head. It was only three questions but they were questions I needed answered to move on from being half way in life and halfway in my head.

After the last meeting of the day, Steele looked at me

"Miss Mills that is the last meeting before I release you for the day, do you still want to talk?" Steele asked

I wanted to yell at the top of my lungs, YES!!!!! Instead I said

"Yes I would please" I said professionally.

"That guy was my brother. My brother has been in and out of rehab since I was a teenager. Mac was released a week ago. Mac has been living with me but a couple days ago I told him that you were working for me." Steele said

"Wait, what do I have to do with your brother" I quickly interrupted him as my heart started to beat 1,000 beats per minute

"When we were younger Mac and I were in a car accident. We hit two parents, two parents of a little girl. That little girl was you" Steele said

I started crying. I thought I was going to pass out. I felt my face become extremely red because I had become so angry. I could barely breathe. I ran out of Steele's office before he could even finish his story. Even though I wanted to know the rest of the story, I couldn't. Steele ruined my life. Everything bad that had happened was because of him and his brother. I ran to the ladies room. I didn't know where else to go at that moment. All I knew was that I didn't want to be in his office with him. Tears wouldn't stop going down my face. I was crying so hard I couldn't breathe. The secret that everyone wanted to know was about me. I only received that job because of what he had done to me. The accident he caused that killed my parents. Why would someone hide that?

It took about an hour but I finally stopped crying. I cleaned myself up. I walked out of the ladies room, Steele stood right by the door. I rolled my eyes.

"I don't ever want to talk to you again. You are the reason my life is the way it is. You ruined my life. I quit." I said

Steele went from looking straight at me to looking down at the floor.

"I understand. I truly am sorry." Steele said

I was walking away when he had said all that. I didn't ever want to think of him again. I went back to my office, grabbed my phone, and then immediately called my Grandma Maggie.

"Hey, I need you to come pick me up." I said

"Okay, I will be there in about 30 minutes" Grandma Maggie said

"Can you hurry? I don't want to be here." I said with irritation in my voice

"I guess, I will try" Grandma Maggie said

"Bye" I said

I hung up the phone before she even had the chance to say goodbye. I started to think about all of the events that had happened in the couple of weeks working for him. My Grandma Maggie had to have known. She was the one that had told me about the job. I heard a knock on the door. It was Steele.

"Can I please come in?" Steele asked

"Seriously, you just told me all that and you still think I want to have any type of conversation with you? I don't ever want to see your face or hear your voice again!" I said with an angry voice.

"I understand, nothing I say will change the past. I just wanted to help. I want you to know the whole truth." Steele said with such regret in his voice.

"I can't handle this right now. Please just let me be." I said very calmly.

I wanted to yell at him so bad but I knew that wouldn't do anything. I wanted to hear the whole story but after I had found the first part of the story, I couldn't take it anymore. I packed up my personal items and started to walk downstairs. Of course there would be Bridgett.

"I told you that you wouldn't last long" Bridgett said

"Bridgett, shut up and go on. Better yet, go be with a killer. He should be in my office." I said

"What are you talking about? Who is the killer in your office?" Bridgett asked

"Oh you didn't know. I thought you knew everything. Steele is a killer." I said with a smart remark.

"Whatever, I am going to see Steele" Bridgett said with a bouncy voice.

"Suit yourself" I said

I stepped in the elevator turned around

"Good luck Bridgett" I said

"Okay bye" Bridgett said with a snarky attitude.

The elevator closed.

Once the elevator reached the first floor, it opened up. I walked out of the elevator. I didn't say a word to anyone. My Grandma Maggie was waiting for me in front of the building. I hopped in the car. I looked right at her.

"Did you know Steele Everest before I received the job?" I asked

"I guess Steele told you" Grandma Maggie said

"That didn't answer my question, did you know Steele before he came to the house?" I asked

"Yes, I met him shortly after the accident. Once Steele started making the money he makes now. Steele started sending us big amounts of money. I became desperate so I called him up to ask if he would give you a job. Steele immediately said yes" Grandma Maggie said

My jaw just dropped. I was flabbergasted.

"We didn't really talk over the years. He would send letters asking about you. In the beginning I didn't respond but he never stopped. It was about a couple months after the accident, I wrote him back. I told him how you were doing and asked how he was doing?" Grandma Maggie said

I just looked at her. I couldn't believe any of this

"Did you let him tell you the whole story?" Grandma Maggie asked

"No, why would I? It isn't going to make me feel any better." I said

"It took me a while to forgive him but it wasn't his fault. It also wasn't good for me to hang on to that anger either." Grandma Maggie said

Grandma Maggie knew everything about the accident.

"I have been blind and lied to my whole life. How can I ever trust anyone ever again" I said

I looked out the car window

"I don't want to talk about this anymore" I said

"Okay that's fine" Grandma Maggie said

The rest of the ride home was quiet. Tears just fell from my eyes the whole way home. I just sat there with my breathing under control, no expression. Just tears falling from my eyes. One drop after another. We finally arrived at the house. I thought to myself, did Steele buy this house for us? What all was a lie? I hopped out of the car and went straight to my bedroom. I laid there for the rest of the night and cried. The guy I thought I was falling for was only in my life because he killed my parents.

The next morning, my Grandma Maggie went to my room.

"The insurance just called. Since your car was totaled, we need to go pick up the new one at the dealership." Grandma Maggie said

I didn't want to go but I needed a car that wasn't that rental.

"Let me finish putting on my clothes and brush my teeth" I said

"Okay, we will need to drive the rental car so we can take it back after we pick up the new car." Grandma Maggie said

I put on some Lululemon leggings and a Nike muscle shirt with a pair of Nike tennis shoes.

"Omg. Okay I will be down shortly." I said

I walked into the bathroom and brushed my teeth. Threw my hair in a messy bun. Great now I have to jump in that stupid rental car. I walked downstairs to jump in that car. We drove to the dealership.

"I am going to have Steele send me the money he has been sending you. Also I'm moving out. I don't want to live with a liar" I said

"Skylan" Grandma Maggie said

I interrupted my Grandma Maggie before she could say anything else

"This isn't a conversation. I'm telling you what is happening and hopefully this will all be done this week." I said with a straight face.

"Okay, I am not going to argue with you" Grandma Maggie said

"Good" I said

Nothing else was said the rest of the way to the dealership. Grandma Maggie hopped out of the car, went into the dealership. She came out with a guy. The guy went to the Tellurides and drove it to where we were parked. I looked at my Grandma Maggie.

"I'm going to Steele's office today" I said

I closed the door, walked over to my new car. Told the man thank you. Jumped in the car. I put my seatbelt on as I thought of the old man, Clinton. I drove out of the dealership parking lot. I had it in my head that I was going straight to Steele's office. I didn't want to face him but I knew I needed to do it. I turned on some country music on the radio. I listened to it until I pulled up to his office. I turned the car off. I sat there for a few minutes before I actually felt like stepping out of the car. When I crawled out of the car, I looked up at Steele's office. Steele was standing, looking out the window. He looked down and looked straight at me. We stared at each other for a few seconds before I walked inside his building. I walked straight to the elevator. Immediately went into the elevator then went directly to the 25 floor. Steele stood at the 25th floor entry of the elevator as he waited for me.

"Miss Mills" Steele said

"Mr. Everest" I said

"Would you like to step into my office?" Steele asked kindly.

"I have come this far, it would be stupid of me to turn around now. Yes." I said

"Good" Steele said with a smile.

"You probably won't like what I am going to say so your smile is more than likely about to disappear." I said

"Okay" Steele said with a confused face.

In the corner of his office Steele had a loveseat and an accent chair. We went over there and sat down.

"Okay Miss Mills, the ball is in your court. What would you like to talk about?" Steele said

My heart was pounding 1,000 beats per minute. I was so nervous, I was surprised I didn't pass out.

"All the money you have been sending my Grandma Maggie. I want it sent to me from now on. I haven't told anyone what you have done. Later on I might want to know the whole story but right now I don't want to be anywhere near you or my Grandma Maggie. You can send me a check or put it into my account. I don't care how we do it but it will be sent to me." I said

"Yes, Miss Mills. Anything" Steele said

"I started to fall in love with you and you broke my heart. I don't want to hear from you until I'm ready. Do you understand?" I said

"Absolutely" Steele said with an upset look.

"How does the money situation work? I have never done anything like this before" I said

"Don't worry about anything, I will take care of everything. When I need you, I will email you. Is that okay?" Steele said

I couldn't figure out if Steele was trying to play me or agreed because he felt guilty.

"Yes, that is fine. Just let me know what all I need to do? Like I said, I have never done anything like this before." I said

As much as I didn't care about the money, I needed him to have some consequence for taking my parents away from me. I missed out on so much because of him and his brother. I thought his brother was dead. Why did Steele tell me that his brother was dead when Mac wasn't? I have multiple questions that I wanted to ask but Steele's face just reminded me of what I lost. Steele lost nothing and I lost everything. I didn't know what to do.

I walked to my car, I didn't exactly know where to go so I went to River Place Nature Trail. I needed to talk to my Grandma Maggie and also Steele but both lied to my face for weeks. My Grandma

110

Maggie lied to me for years. Steele had lied to me since I started working for him.

Once I arrived at River Place Nature Trail, I just sat in the parking lot. I didn't know what to do or where to go. I sat in the parking lot and cried. I felt betrayed. Everyone lied to me for years. Until recently I didn't talk about my parents. It wasn't that I never thought of them, I just never said anything out loud. My Grandma Maggie and I just never talked about them.

Every elephant tear that came from my eyes made me think of all the memories with my parents and Steele. I couldn't hold it back anymore. I cried more than I had in years. One teardrop after another led to another memory after another. I sat my hands on the steering wheel. I looked in from where I saw beautiful land but I couldn't stay looking at it. I put my head on my hands. All the elephant tears just fell like it was pouring down raining. Steele, the guy I started to fall for and Grandma Maggie, the only family I had left became the two people I couldn't trust anymore. The deep lies that were kept for years. I tried my hardest to stop the tears but the harder I tried the harder it was to stop.

It took about two hours but I finally stopped. I felt as though I had cried enough to fill a pond. All the pain and betrayal was still there. I knew I needed to find a place to live but I only had a few hundred to my name. I went to the Embassy Suites by Hilton Austin Central. I had no clue what to do, my body felt weak but also numb. Even though my body had released out every endorphin that it needed to, the pain was still there. My eyes looked terrible and my makeup was everywhere. I had cried so much that my mascara was nonexistent to my eyelashes. My eyes looked like Carrie Underwood's Cry Pretty eyes but instead of glitter it was black. I didn't know the next step from where I was.

Once I arrived in the room at Embassy Suites I decided to pull out my phone. I started to look up apartments and house rentals in Austin, Texas. I knew I wanted to stay in Austin because even though my life was turned upside down, Austin was still my parents' home. I needed to stay there for them. It was the last place that I could hold on to my parents.

All of the places were expensive. I didn't realize how expensive apartments and houses were at the time. I had looked at apartments and houses for hours. That evening Steele emailed me. I couldn't believe the email after I read it.

"I called your grandma, she said you are not home. Can you please email me back just so I know you are okay?

Steele Everest

CEO of Everest Corp

Email: SteeleEverest@everestcorp.com

Phone number: 858-345-1633"

The email said

I wanted to reply to tell him off and yell through an email instead I said

"I have been looking at apartments and houses. I didn't realize how much they cost. You and my Grandma Maggie lied to me. I can't excuse the pain and ignorance that I have received from those lies. I just can't. I am okay. I am staying at a hotel.

-Skylan Mills" I wrote back in an email

I shocked myself because I felt as though I wrote it with such poise and honesty

"I will help you in any way you will let me, I understand I should have met you a long time ago. I can't bring your parents back but I am here to help. I will buy you a house or apartment of your choice if you would like. All I ask is for you to let me know that you are okay.

Steele Everest

CEO of Everest Corp

Email: SteeleEverest@everestcorp.com

Phone number: 888-345-1633" Steele emailed

I didn't know what to say at that moment. I was extremely disappointed, frustrated and exhausted. I put my phone down and laid down on the bed. I thought about his offer. I knew he did it out of guilt. I had truly considered his offer, I knew I wouldn't be able to afford anything I honestly wanted. I fell asleep shortly after my head hit my pillow.

I woke up the next morning around 8 AM. I heard the maid knock on the door. I told her I was still in the room. She left but I didn't go back to sleep like normal. I looked at my phone. I had many missed calls, text messages and emails from my Grandma Maggie and Steele.

I decided to put them in a group message to make it easier for me.

"I am still okay. I went to sleep and just woke up. Calm down." I texted in the group message to Steele and my Grandma Maggie.

I immediately received a text back from both of them.

"That's good" Steele texted

"Call me" my Grandma Maggie texted

I thought about it for about 5 minutes before I decided I would call her. Ultimately, I will need to talk to both of them at some point.

I decided to call her.

"Where are you at?" Grandma Maggie asked

"Embassy Suites in Austin" I said

"When are you coming home?" Grandma Maggie asked

"You are joking right?" I asked

"Does it sound like I am joking? I am concerned and we need to talk about everything" Grandma Maggie said

Concerned...I didn't even know that was in her vocabulary

I just don't understand how both of them lied to me. I deserved to know that I was working for my parent's killer.

"I don't know when I will be back to your house, I do know that I will no longer be living with you" I said

"We need to talk whether it's at home or in a coffee shop" Grandma Maggie said with remorse.

I could hear the weight of the pain she had but my pain hurt just as much. I didn't know how to handle the pain that I was dealt at that moment.

"Whatever, I will text you and let you know by tonight. I need to think about it." I said

"Okay that sounds good. I will be watching out for your text" Grandma Maggie said

As soon as I hung up the phone with her, I called Steele. My hands were sweaty. My heart was pumping so fast that I knew I was about to have a panic attack. I didn't want to call him, for crying out loud I was falling in love with the guy. Everything had changed. It's not like I could've just asked anyone. What does a person do when they fall in love with their parent's killer? Would a therapist have any advice on this? It's not like it happened every day!

I tried to be as calm as possible. The phone started to ring, my stomach felt like it was going to drop out of my body!

It rang 2 times, I almost hung up because I didn't want to actually talk to him.

"Hello Miss Skylan Mills. Thank you for calling me!" Steele answered the phone completely differently than my Grandma Maggie did. It was strange.

"Hello, Steele" I said

"I am surprised that you called me. I figured that you would ignore me. Thank you for calling" Steele said

"You're welcome, we can talk. I accept your offer on the house. When are you free to talk? Does a lawyer need to be present to do all the stuff that we need to finish?" I said

"Yes. I can call my lawyer. Have you looked at any place you want to live?" Steele said

"I have looked around but nothing is set in stone. I will probably look around some more." I said

"Okay, let me call you back. I will call my lawyer." Steele said

"Okay, I assume you already have done this with my Grandma Maggie." I said

"Sort of. I would just send a check in the mail and ask how you were doing." Steele said

"Okay, just give me a call back" I said

"Okay, talk to you soon" Steele said, happier than I definitely was at the moment.

"Bye" I said

The call ended, while I waited on the call back I started to look at houses and apartments. I found one that was nice and I could live in it forever. It was expensive. I might have gone over the price range out of spite but I didn't care. It was 2 million dollars. 7 bedrooms and 5 bathrooms, I was in awe of the house. Everything about it was beautiful. I decided that house was the one.

Even though I didn't look that long, at least I had something for the lawyer. Two million dollars was a bunch of money, Steele was the one who said he would buy me a house. I hoped so much that the house I chose would fit the budget. I wondered if I even had a budget. I wondered if Steele was falling for me and that's the reason he told me. Maybe he just felt guilty. I didn't want to be around Steele because he hurt me. At the same time I did want to be around Steele. I was confused and stupid. I didn't know how to react to it all. I was just going through the motions of what I was feeling at that given moment.

I wanted to drive to my Grandma Maggie's to lay in my bed and watch TV. She was at work so it was possible. I jumped on my phone to the Find My app. Her location was turned off. I decided to risk it, Steele hadn't called me back yet. I needed to check out of the hotel.

I walked downstairs to check out, Steele was downstairs in the lobby. I wondered how long he had been waiting down there.

"Do you want to go grab something to eat?" Steele asked

"Why?" I asked

"Because breakfast is the most important meal of the day" Steele said

That was the best answer he could come up with at the moment

"Steele, why are you here?" I asked

"I wanted to talk before all the lawyers. I would like to tell my whole story" Steele said

I didn't know if I wanted to hear his story but I decided to be civil. After all, Steele was buying me a house.

"Okay. You are buying" I said

"Deal. Where do you want to go?" Steele interrupted me.

"You are the food expert in this room, not me. You pick" I said

Steele always picked the best place. If it was anything other than food then Steele would insist on me picking. Steele picked a place called Josephine House. It was expensive but he had the money to pay for it.

We walked into the restaurant, of course we were seated right away. I guess it helped that I was with a billionaire.

"Okay, now that we are here and sitting down, go on with your story" I said

"I am telling you this because you deserve the truth" Steele said

"My brother was at a college party. He told me to come pick him up. So I decided to hop in my car and go pick him up. I heard that he had been drinking so I didn't want him to drive. My brother Mac, told me the address so I jumped in my car then drove to campus as soon as I could. As soon as I pulled up I walked in to find my brother. Then Mac demanded the keys so even though I didn't want to give the keys to Mac, he snatched them out of my hands. We jumped in the car, the next moment I knew we were about halfway home when we were driving across a bridge. There was a couple, who were parents. They were going home to their daughter. My brother and I argued over him driving while he was drunk…"

I interrupted Steele while he was telling me the story

"Now wait, how do I know you are not lying to me right now. You told me your brother died?" I said

"Mac didn't literally die but I completely lost him that night" Steele said

"Okay. Whatever" I said

"Can I proceed?" Steele said

"Yes you may" I said

"I kept telling him to let me drive. Mac looked at me to yell at me about driving drunk. In the midst of the argument we hit the car with the parents of a little girl. It was the first time he had taken the keys from me and drove drunk. I suppose the other times we were just lucky. I'm not sure. I was hurt but not that bad. It didn't do much to my brother but the parents, your parents passed away before the ambulance arrived at the wreck. I wanted to know everything I could about it. I figured out the life and family of the two people in the wreck. Mac's sentence was 18 years, he was released early from prison on good behavior." Steele said

"Why didn't you tell me all of this before he was released from prison?" I said with frustration.

"I didn't think he would go around you" Steele said with remorse.

"Okay, finish" I said

"Okay, I told him that you were working for me. When I first began writing to your grandmother, my brother didn't want to know anything about you. As time went on my brother finally asked about you. Every time I would hear new information about you then I would tell him. I didn't think that Mac would go as far as coming up to you in a parking lot. I am sure he just wanted to talk to you. Even though the accident happened 13 years ago, we still wanted to keep tabs on you. We wanted to make sure you were okay and well taken care of. Since I was asking about you frequently she finally asked me if I wanted to go to one of your sporting events. She sent me an announcement for your high school and college graduation. Since you were about 10 is when I started going to all your sporting events and school activities" Steele said

"Wait, you were at my high school and college graduation and all competitions?" I asked

When I was younger I was in gymnastics so it took a bunch of my time up so I can only imagine how much time it took up for him. I knew Steele was at some but I didn't know he was at all of my competitions.

"Yes, overtime your grandmother informed me on all the events. I always made it a priority to go to each event." Steele said

My thoughts were all over the place. Steele has been around the majority of my life. My Grandma Maggie never even told me that Steele asked about me. It started to make sense why I was accepted for the job so quickly and easily.

"What is the reason you haven't had a girlfriend in 13 years? That number matches up with your brother's prison time" I said

"Between my company and you, I haven't had the time" Steele said

So I was part of the reason Steele was the most eligible bachelor in America. That was comforting to know that I was the reason.

"What happened to the girl from high school?" I asked

"I didn't have time. My ex was frustrated with me after the wreck. I had changed so much my ex didn't like it. I wasn't making much time for her." Steele said

"Okay" I said

"If you don't mind me asking...what has been going on here recently?" Steele asked

"My life took a turn after college. I didn't have school or sports anymore." I said depressed

"Your grandmother said that you two have been fighting more than usual here in the past couple years. Do you mind telling me about it?" Steele asked

"Did my Grandma Maggie ask you to ask me that?" I said

"No, I just wanted to know what has been happening. I haven't heard much about you recently. When your Grandma Maggie asked me if I would hire you, my immediate response was YES. You graduated with honors in business so of course I would say yes" Steele said

"Oh really? Thanks I guess" I said

"Yes, I had never met you. I always kept my distance from you. When you Grandma Maggie asked if I would give you a job, I couldn't say no. I had always wanted to meet you but I didn't want to interrupt your life. Why didn't you receive any offers after you graduated?" Steele said

"Actually I received an abundance of offers. I worked for a place for about 2 months. It caused me to go into deeper depression so much I didn't want to go to work. Eventually, I just quit going altogether. I have been dealing with bad depression. I am taking care of it now" I said

Of course it wasn't my plan to tell Steele that I had depression but he knew everything else about me

"I didn't know that. I'm really sorry" Steele said like I had another death in my family

119

"Where is your brother now?" I asked

Since apparently Steele didn't kill my parents, his brother did. I didn't exactly know how to feel about all the information that Steele told me. He knew more about me than I could imagine. How does someone take all that information and not freak out about it? It was all too much for me. I was surprised that I didn't have an anxiety attack right there in the restaurant.

"A few years ago I bought a place in New York. I fly there often so I decided to buy a place. I sent him there. I didn't want him to be around you. You might not care for me but I do care for you. Since that wreck happened. Over the years I have come to deeply care for you. I would never want anything bad to happen to you. I would never want you to be scared of a man coming up to your car." Steele said

"Are you joking? He should be back in prison for coming up to me!" I said

"I understand that you don't like him? He has given you no reason for you to like him" Steele said

"He looked drunk and homeless" I said

"Yes, he was drunk. Not homeless but drunk was definitely a word you could use." Steele said

It was all unbelievable. I couldn't fathom the knowledge that I had received in that past hour. Steele had kept tabs on me for the past 13 years.

"I am still thinking about you watching me for the past 13 years" I said

"When you say it like that, it makes it sound like I was a stalker." Steele said

"Umm well you kind of are" I said

"I wouldn't say that considering I was invited by your Grandma Maggie every time. I never came if I wasn't invited" Steele said

120

"I can't believe you have been keeping all of this from me for years." I said

"I wanted to tell you and I almost did when you were 18 but I changed my mind. I decided I didn't want to mess up your life" Steele said

"I'm probably crossing a line but I have secretly been crushing on you for the past few years. It only became worse when you hired me. My head is so confused it doesn't know, up from down right now. My heart is so mad at you that it doesn't want anything to do with you!" I said

"I'm sorry. I guess we will be crossing the line. I am falling in love with you. The past few weeks have been amazing. You took my heart. When you were younger I saw the ambition and strive you had. I cared for you but the past few weeks the care I had for you has changed into a deeper, different care. It wasn't this little girl I wanted to meet anymore. It was a woman that still held that ambition and strive. A woman who can move mountains and waterfalls if she wants. There is so much I see in you. I can't remember the feelings I had before I actually met you but now nothing means anything as long as you are happy." Steele said passionately.

My mouth dropped and my eyes went wide. My stomach dropped and if I wouldn't have been in a chair then I would have fallen to the ground. My heart was beating faster than it ever had before. None of it could be real. He had fallen in love with me. It was not possible. Could it be possible?

"Okay, are you saying this so you don't have to give me money or why are you telling me all of this?" I said

"Absolutely not. I wouldn't ever lie about that." Steele said

Steele had lied and hid information from me for years. How could I trust anything that had come from Steele's mouth?

"This is all unbelievable, you realize how crazy this sounds?" I said

"Yes, I understand but I figured that you deserve to know" Steele said

"Of course this would be the perfect moment to tell me" I said

"I needed to explain myself." Steele said

"Okay, so what are you expecting me to say or do now?" I said

"I suppose whatever you want to do. I don't want you to quit, if you want your job back then it's yours. Honestly you deserve whatever you want." Steele said

How was I supposed to argue with someone who would give me the world?

"Whatever?" I said

"Whatever, you don't know how much my life had changed when the wreck happened. I didn't think it could change anymore. Then you actually came into my life. It hasn't been the same" Steele said

"Are you saying this because your lawyer isn't here" I said as I crossed my arms

"Absolutely not" Steele said

My heart and mind wasn't on the same page.

"I'm going to need to think about all this. Can we have a meeting with the lawyers tomorrow?" I asked

"Yes we can" Steele said

"Okay, can we finish eating? Are you done eating?" I asked

"Yes I am. Are you?" Steele asked

"Yes" I said

Steele had already paid for the food. It was really good. Just like I figured it would be.

"Alright, where do you want me to take you?" Steele asked

"I guess take me to my Grandma Maggie's house. I need to talk to her." I said

"Okay." Steele said

We stood up then walked out. Mr. Busch waited for us in the front of the restaurant. Steele opened the door for me which I always thought was strange because I figured that Mr. Busch would do it. Mr. Busch opened the door for Steele, I never knew why Steele always opened the door for me. I guess I figured it out that day.

"Did you like the food?" Steele asked

Apparently, Steele thought that he could have changed the conversation to small talk after an intense conversation. That wasn't going to happen, I never would have imagined the conversation with my boss would end in the confession of keeping tabs on me my whole life.

"Do you like the weather?" I asked with sarcasm.

"Okay, so no small talk" Steele said

"I need a minute to take in everything you told me. I wasn't expecting to find out all that information all before my day actually started so thanks for that" I said with a sarcastic tone

"You are absolutely right, I shouldn't speculate that we could have small talk after that intense talk" Steele said

"Thanks for finally comprehending that after I had to throw it in your face" I said

"I'm sorry." Steele said

"It's fine" I said

Even though it wasn't fine. Steele should have known that I didn't want to talk anymore. He had just thrown a bomb of information at me.

"Really" Steele said

"Yes really" I said

No, no, no, no. It was not fine.

"Okay" Steele said

"Okay" I said

Since small talk was out of the question we ended up sitting there until we arrived at my Grandma Maggie's house.

"Let me open your door please" Steele said

"I can open my own door. Stay here. I need to take it from here." I said

"Are you sure?" Steele asked

"Absolutely" I said

I stepped out of the vehicle. I walked up to the front door. The emotions I felt were almost too overwhelming. As I stood there and stared at the front door. It took me back to a memory of the house that I lived in when I was little. The house that my parents lived in before they died. I lived in an old Victorian home. It was in Austin. 617 Blanco Street, Austin, Texas to be exact. I will never forget the address. When I received my driver's license I drove by there every night. I used to go by there all the time. I haven't been there in a few years but I still think of some of the memories I had when I was there.

After I would go to bed they would walk out on the front porch. They had this old radio that they brought outside for music every night. I would watch them dance for what seemed like hours. It didn't matter what the weather was each night. Every night I would sneak downstairs and peek out the window. Every night my parents would be outside on the porch dancing like it was their honeymoon night. The smile on my mom's face was priceless. She was so beautiful. Her smile could light up an entire room. She had the prettiest smile and the prettiest teeth that made a person want to stare at them all day long. The way my dad looked at her was exceptional. I had never experienced a man's exceptional stare at me like I was the whole world and I was the only woman in it. I had never looked at a man that made me smile so big that it lit up the room. I wanted a love like theirs with every fiber in my body. A person would be crazy to not want a love like theirs. It was simple but elegant. When I imagined my husband, it was someone who stood out on the porch with me while our kids were secretly at the window watching us dance to our song.

I wanted so badly for Steele to be the one I danced on the front porch with.

After all of the feelings and past came out, I had changed my mind. I started to think I would never receive the gaze that my mom received from my dad. I think the best one was when she was reading a book. She would be so deep into the book. The gaze my dad gave my mom was a sight I haven't seen anyone make since they were alive. My parents truly loved each other unconditionally. It was more inspiring than any movie I had ever seen.

Steele was only being nice out of guilt. He should have done a better job at keeping the keys from his brother the night of the wreck. We all wouldn't have been in this life if he had just kept the keys. My parents wouldn't be dead. All he had to do was keep the keys from his brother. I never understood how he could let him just take the keys. If he wasn't drunk and his brother was then how did it actually happen?

I walked in the house. My Grandma Maggie was in the living room. I guessed that she didn't go to work that day. I was at her house before she usually arrived home from work. She came straight up to me and hugged me as tight as she could. It was strange, she hadn't done that in years.

"You don't need to leave. You are all I have" Grandma Maggie said

As I pull away from her hug

"We need to talk" I said

"Of course, what do you want to know?" Grandma Maggie asked

"Your side of the story. Steele just told me his side but obviously yours is going to be different." I said

"Yes, of course. I don't know everything about the wreck. Of course Steele will know more about that but I can tell you about the time after the wreck." Grandma Maggie said

"Yes, I understand that." I said

"The week of the wreck there was a bunch I had to deal with, it took a while for me to receive the police report. I know they died on the scene, the other two survived. A few weeks after the wreck, Steele reached out in a letter. It didn't respond right away. I still have all the letters that he sent me. If you want I can give them to you. Each one of them is kind and sincere. I knew you would want to read them someday so I kept them. I was going to tell you about them when you graduated high school but I could never find the right time." Grandma Maggie said

"Anytime would have been a good time" I interrupted

"You are correct. It took me a month to write him back. I didn't want to do it at first but Steele had sent me another letter. Each letter has his phone number and email address. I met Steele for coffee one time when you were at a friend's house. We met, I didn't realize he was a minor at the time. It took me months to receive the police report but it explained so much. He was very kind and polite when we talked. He seemed troubled by the whole situation. He had asked to meet you one time when you were in Jr. High but I didn't think it would be a good idea at the time. After we met, Steele still wrote letters and asked about you. Every school activity and meet you had, I would invite him. Steele always showed up, I was very impressed. Steele never missed any event. If I couldn't make it, I knew that Steele would write me a letter after the event later. There was not one time that Steele missed. I tried to tell Steele multiple times that he could meet you but I never could go through with it." Grandma Maggie said

"I never realized that he was at every meet, both graduations and every school function. I did notice Steele was at a few of them. When

I was in Jr. High school Steele became my crush. I didn't realize that Steele was at every event of mine. I just knew that I had seen him at some of my meets." I said

"You never told me that you had a crush on him before you started to work for him." Grandma Maggie said

"We haven't been close in years. It was just a crush, I wasn't in love with him yet." I said

"Yet, so now you are in love with him?" Grandma Maggie asked

"I don't know. After I have learned all of this, I don't know" I said

"Have you talked to him about this?" Grandma Maggie asked

"Doesn't matter. Just go on with the rest of the story" I said

"The day that I called you about the job, I called him early that morning. I needed you to start working. Steele had financially given me more money and support than anyone could ask for. This time I called Steele up and asked if he could give you a job. Steele didn't hesitate for one moment. I think Steele was excited that I had finally asked him to do something for you. Also Steele had never met you and I am sure he was excited about that too." Grandma Maggie said

"Okay I don't know how I haven't had an anxiety attack today. All of this information is overwhelming." I said

"Okay, I think it would be best for you to read the letters. I figured that it would be easier. I kept them in the back of my closet so that you would never find them. Clearly I don't have the ones I wrote, maybe you can ask Steele for those letters. If you have any questions then you can come ask me. I will be completely open with you about all of it" Grandma Maggie said

She pulled a box out from under the coffee table. In the box there were many letters rubber banded together. I was in awe of how many letters there were.

"Here you go, I hope this helps you" Grandma Maggie said

"All of these letters are from him?" I asked

"Every single one of these letters are from him" Grandma Maggie said

"This is incredible. You saved every single one of them" I said

"I figured this day would come sooner or later. I thought you might want to read them yourself." Grandma Maggie said

Well she wasn't wrong. I just didn't think there would be so many of them. I gave her a hug and a kiss on the check

"Thank you. I will be in my room, I really need to read these. I have a meeting with the lawyers tomorrow with Steele. I need to make up my mind but I need to read these first." I said

"You're welcome. I'm off for the next few days so I'm here if you need me" Grandma Maggie said

I picked the box up. Dang, it was heavy. I carried them up to my room. My Grandma Maggie organized them by year so I started from the beginning.

19

NINETEEN deep breaths

Hello Mrs. Maggie Mills

My name is Steele Everest. I was one of the guys that was in the wreck that your son and daughter-in-law was involved in. First, I want to apologize for the death of your son and daughter-in-law. If you haven't figured it out by now, my brother was driving and I was in the passenger seat. We were arguing and it went too far. My brother looked away from the road for a short period of time. When we realized we were about to hit another car it was too late. I want to also apologize on my brother's behalf in part for the accident as well. I am sure you are still very busy with everything that is going on. If you need help with anything feel free to reach out. My family and I will help as much as we can. Again, I am very sorry for your loss. You may contact me through my email or phone number. If you would like, you can send a letter back if you are more comfortable communicating that way. My phone number is 555-456-4569 and my email is steeledog4@hotmail.com.

Have a nice day

June 4, 2008

Letter I

Steele Everest

As I sat there reading the first letter, my eyes started to water. The words on the letter started to become blurry. I held the letter a little away from my face so I wouldn't have tears on the letters. I had to make a short laugh at his email address. steeledog4@hotmail.com

The moment I was reading the first letter, my Grandma Maggie walked in the room. She didn't say anything, she sat a glass of water down on my bedside table then walked out.

My heart was so heavy that I decided to take a breather for a moment. I didn't think the first letter would have such a big impact on me but it did. I took a drink of the glass of water that my Grandma Maggie had sat on my bedside table.

It was so hard to read the first letter that I almost stopped reading the letters but I knew I needed to read them. It would determine the actions I make tomorrow and in the future. I picked up the second letter.

Hello Mrs. Maggie Mills,

My name is Steele Everest. I was in the car accident that involved your son and daughter-in-law. I want to send my sincere apologies. I am not sure if you received the first letter I mailed to you. I want to help but I don't know how to help. I heard your grandchild is living with you. I understand it's not much but here is a check for 100 dollars to help you out with whatever you need help on. Please feel free to email or call me anytime. If that isn't enough for you then you are more than welcome to mail a letter back if you please. My email address is steeledog4@hotmail.com. My phone number 555-456-4569.

Have a great day

June 9, 2008

Letter II

Steele Everest

P.S. How is your granddaughter doing?

Two down a million to go. My heart felt like it was about to pop out of my chest. My eyes were so watery I could barely read. My nose ran so much I had to sit up to grab some Kleenex. I looked at the next box of letters for a few minutes. I thought about the tears that had already fallen down my cheeks and hit my shirt.

Hello Mrs. Maggie Mills,

Thank you for writing me back. I understand there wasn't much money but I hope it will help you in some way. Thank you for keeping your granddaughter, I am sure it's not easy to do. I heard you are not married so you are having to do it alone. I am sorry about that. It is one of the reasons I want to help if I can. If you ever want to meet for coffee or whatever I am up for that but only if you are willing to meet. I don't want you to feel obligated to do so. Please cash the check.

July 1, 2008

Letter III

Steele Everest

P.S. How is your granddaughter doing?

I wondered if she met him because he gave her money. I did have questions that she needed to answer before the meeting. I picked up another letter. I looked at the envelope, it was stamped July 22, 2008. I took a deep breath and opened the next letter.

Hello Mrs. Maggie Mills

Thank you for meeting with me. It was a pleasure meeting you. Your granddaughter is lucky to have you. My grandma died when I was three years old so I didn't really know her. Thank you for trying to buy my coffee that day. I am wondering how you and Skylan are doing? I hope all is well considering your loss. Thank you for finally taking the money. It will all be worth it one day.

July 22, 2008

Letter IV

Steele Everest

P.S. If you ever decide you want to email me or call me. My email is *steeledog4@hotmail.com* *or my cell phone number is 555-456-4569*

Even though the letters so far weren't long, it was emotionally difficult to read. I had to take a drink of water before I could even look at another envelope, much less comprehend words on paper. By the time I was on my fifth letter my eyes were puffy and red.

Hello Mrs. Maggie Mills,

Thank you for the letter. I can only give 50 dollars right now. In the next letter I will send you more. Thank you for the invitation to Skylan's competition. I have never been to a gymnastics meet before so it will definitely be interesting to watch. I definitely won't know what is going on but I will be looking for Skylan. Thank you for the picture you sent in the last letter. Even though she won't know I'm there supporting her on her parents behalf I'm still honored that I am invited. I understand I'm not her parents, not that I could take that spot. I'm just grateful that you invited me to her competition. How is she doing with school and everything?

August 5, 2008

Letter V

Steele Everest

P.S. If you ever decide you want to email me or call me. My email is *steeledog4@hotmail.com* *or my cell phone number is 555-456-4569*

My Grandma Maggie gave him a picture. She better have looked into Steele before she sent him a picture of me.

I walked down the stairs. I was out of water plus I needed a break.

My Grandma Maggie was sitting on the couch watching TV.

"I am going to fill my cup up with more water. We need to talk about the letters and what was sent in them." I said

"Okay, I told you that I would be open with you" Grandma Maggie said

I walked into the kitchen and went to the refrigerator. I stuck my cup in the space under the inlet valve for some ice in the ice maker. I filled it up halfway with ice and pushed the water button. Then I filled the cup up with water. I walked into the living room and sat down on the couch.

I took a drink of my water then gently sat it down on the coffee table.

"I'm at letter five. You gave him a picture of me. What did you do with the money? Did he ever sit with you at any of my events? It seems that you two knew each other very well. What all did you talk about at that first meeting of yours" I said

"I guess Steele had your car brought back here because it's outside. The first picture of you was with your parents. It was one of the family photos that was taken before the wreck. Your vehicles and your college were paid with that money. We talked about a variety of topics at that meeting. I tried to give him that check back at that meeting. We came to an agreement with the money. Steele would send me money and I would put it in your savings account. We didn't live off his money if that is what you were thinking. I figured it would stop but thirteen years later Steele is still sending money." Grandma Maggie said

"So Steele paid for my college and my cars?" I said

"Yes" Grandma Maggie said

"That is all the questions I have for now. I'm going back to my room to keep reading" I said

"Okay I will be down here" Grandma Maggie said

I grabbed my glass of water and walked back up the stairs.

Hello Mrs. Maggie Mills

Wow! I saw so much ambition in Skylan, your grand-daughter at the meet. Thank you for inviting me. She looks like she works really hard in that sport. There is no way I could do that. She has so much strength. Even if she doesn't know it now she has so much strength, strive and motivation. It was inspiring to watch. Hopefully everything will get better with this school year. She does have a bunch going on in her life. I'm not sure if this will help you but this all changed my life for the better. Thank you for writing to me. It means a lot to me. Thank you for keeping me informed on Skylan. I appreciate you doing that.

I wrote a check for 100 dollars, just like we agreed on.

August 22, 2008

Letter VI

Steele Everest

P.S. If you ever decide you want to email me or call me. My email is steeledog4@hotmail.com *or my cell phone number is 555-456-4569*

I smile, take a deep breath. I picked up another one.

Hello Mrs. Maggie Mills,

I'm happy to know the first day of school went better than expected. My mom would take the first day of school pictures too. They were goofy when my brother and I were little. We never liked taking pictures. The older we became the more the pictures looked like we hated the world. I always hated pictures but my mom always made us take them. This year is the last year for school pictures. I decided for my mom that I would smile for her this year, since it is my last. She won't be there for college next year. I hope you keep the tradition going with her. I bet it's different this year. I knew they were in the education field. I just didn't know that you took them every year.

Here is a check for 135 dollars. I decided to accept a job that pays well. Plus I told my parents what I am doing now. They approve of it. They think it will teach me to have better character. Also help me stay out of trouble.

September 7, 2008

Letter VII

Steele Everest

P.S. If you ever decide you want to email me or call me. My email is steeledog4@hotmail.com *or my cell phone number is 555-456-4569*

Dang, Steele worked a job just to put money into my savings account. He must have felt really bad about the wreck. I never knew my Grandma Maggie had a savings account for me. I wondered if there was any money in there since Steele kept sending money after I graduated college. I could have already had my own place. What the heck Grandma Maggie?

Hello Mrs. Maggie Mills,

Hope you are having a good week. How is Skylan doing? How are you doing? Hope all is well with you. I went to another competition. I don't know if you were there or not. I just wanted to tell you that your granddaughter is amazing at gymnastics. I don't know much about it but it looks like she is doing a good job. Just like I promised I wrote you a check. Thank you so much for putting the money in a savings account for Skylan. I am grateful that you are putting it in a good place.

September 29, 2008

Letter VIII

Steele Everest

P.S. If you ever decide you want to email me or call me. My email is steeledog4@hotmail.com *or my cell phone number is 555-456-4569*

Hello Mrs. Maggie Mills,

Hope everything is still going great with you and Skylan. How is she doing in school? I know the school year just started. I hope that she is doing well with her education. I can tell she is doing awesome in her gymnastics. I have gone to every competition that you have sent me. I wish I had that much energy and strength. Just like promised there is a check in the envelope that has the money to put into Skylan's savings account. Thank you again for letting me contribute to it.

October 13, 2008

Letter IX

Steele Everest

P.S. If you ever decide you want to email me or call me. My email is steeledog4@hotmail.com or my cell phone number is 555-456-4569

Hello Mrs. Maggie Mills,

It's good to hear that y'all are doing well. I hope she is still working hard on gymnastics. She seems better and better the more time goes on. Has she always been that good at gymnastics? I never went to a meet until I watched Skylan. The strength a person needs to do the stunts a person needs to do for one event of the sport is incredible. I am always here if you ever need anything. I don't know if you and Skylan are going to celebrate Halloween this year but Happy Halloween.

October 28, 2008

Letter X

Steele Everest

P.S. If you ever decide you want to email me or call me. My email is steeledog4@hotmail.com or my cell phone number is 555-456-4569

Hello Mrs. Maggie Mills,

Thank you for asking about me. I am doing well. I am happy that you are still writing to me. I went to another one of Skylan's meets. It looks like she is doing great in gymnastics. How is she doing with school? Do you need any more money? Are you doing okay with finances? I decided to start my own business. It is doing very well. I can send you more money if you would like me to, you can put it in her savings account or you can use it for whatever you feel is best. I wrote a check for the 100 dollars we agreed on to put in Skylan's savings account. You can use some of it for Thanksgiving if you would like or put it in her savings account. Happy Thanksgiving to you and Skylan.

November 15, 2008

Letter XI

Steele Everest

P.S. If you ever decide you want to email me or call me. My email is steeledog4@hotmail.com or my cell phone number is 555-456-4569

Those letters were hard to read. It was like taking a knife to my heart. It was a pain that I never had endured before. I wished that I could have skipped the pain I had that week.

Hello Mrs. Maggie Mills,

I am happy to know that you two are doing good or as good as can be expected. My business is really growing. Do you want to meet up soon? We can change our agreements. If not then you can just keep writing to me. We can do whatever you please. Thank you again for inviting me to all of Skylan's meets. I wish that her parents could be there. It might not mean much to you but this changed me as a person. Before the accident I didn't think of anyone but myself. I put a little more money on the check than usual. Skylan will need it more than me.

November 30, 2008

Letter XII

Steele Everest

P.S. If you ever decide you want to email me or call me. My email is <u>*steeledog4@hotmail.com*</u> *or my cell phone number is 555-456-4569*

Everything that Steele wrote in the letters made me want to bawl to the point I couldn't breathe. I could barely take it. The time Steele took and the money he gave my Grandma Maggie made my heart hurt so much. The effort and emotion that Steele put into each letter made me happy and sympathetic. I could tell that Steele meant every word in the letters. I could feel the pain he felt from the accident. Even though he didn't lose anyone in the accident. The letters showed me that it did change him in a good way. I wished I didn't feel the pain that Steele endured because it felt like losing my parents all over again.

Hello Mrs. Maggie Mills,

I am doing great. Thank you very much for asking. The business is doing great so that helps with our money solution. I hope that you and Skylan have a great Christmas. I did leave you a little extra on the check for Christmas or whatever. If you want to put it in Skylan's savings account, I understand that too. I understand that you don't want to meet up. I will always try my best to respect your wants and wishes. I never want to make it feel like you can't trust me or that I am overstepping my bounds. If we meet up again I want you to feel comfortable. I also don't want to make you feel as though you are obligated to meet up with me either. How is Skylan doing? Is she doing okay with school? Is she looking forward to Christmas? I hope all is going well. I understand this will be her first Christmas without her parents so I hope she still enjoys it. She is really lucky to have you. She probably doesn't even realize it either.

December 9, 2008

Letter XIII

Steele Everest

P.S. If you ever decide you want to email me or call me. My email is steeledog4@hotmail.com or my cell phone number is 555-456-4569

Hello Mrs. Maggie Mills,

How are you and Skylan doing? I hope life is treating both of you well. I can't believe this year is almost over. I hope the extra money I am giving you for Skylan isn't offending you. I would never want to do that. If you need anything else, I will do my best to provide you with it. The past few months that I have been writing to you show me how much independence you have for yourself and for your granddaughter. I can tell the amount of strength you obtain. Skylan is lucky to have such a strong and independent grandma. I hope the both of you are doing well. Merry Christmas and Happy New Year! I left more money than we agreed on. I hope that is okay. If you want we can change our agreement.

December 23, 2008

Letter XIV

Steele Everest

P.S. If you ever decide you want to email me or call me. My email is steeledog4@hotmail.com or my cell phone number is 555-456-4569

I sat the letter down on my nightstand. I walked to the window in my bedroom. I looked out the window while thinking to myself, was it all real? I couldn't believe the words that I had read or the million letters left that I still hadn't read. My stomach felt like I was going to throw up. My eyes were buffy from all the tears that ran down my face. My heart was aching so much I couldn't relax to save my life. It took all my strength to stand on my two legs. I felt like at any moment my legs would give out. I felt as if I would fall to the ground at any moment. I didn't have much energy. I needed to finish reading those letters but at the same time all I wanted to do was fall down on my bed and cry. I wanted to act like Steele and my Grandma Maggie didn't betray me. I wanted to wake up tomorrow and go to work like my boss and my Grandma Maggie hadn't lied to me my whole life. I walked back over to my bed, picked up the next letter. I took a deep breath, closed my eyes and opened the next letter.

Hello Mrs. Maggie Mills,

I am happy to hear that you both had nice holidays. I hope Skylan received everything that she wanted. I am sure she wanted her parents there. I wish I could change that for you and for her. I am sorry again for what happened to you. I understand that pain will never completely go away for you and Skylan. You are both amazing people, I am sorry that the accident happened to incredible people. No one deserves to lose their children. No one deserves to lose their parents at such a young age. I am happy that she has you at least. Thank you for accepting the extra money. Thank you for putting the money into her savings account. Thank you for writing me back. I hope this year is better than last year. I left the check in the envelope. I am okay with keeping the amount agreement and just sending extra money when I can.

January 26, 2009

Letter XV

Steele Everest

P.S. If you ever decide you want to email me or call me. My email is steeledog4@hotmail.com *or my cell phone number is 555-456-4569*

Hello Mrs. Maggie Mills,

I hope your year is going well. I can't believe it's February. I went to Skylan's meet this weekend. I tried not to yell too loud to respect that you don't want us to meet right now. I have been reading about gymnastics to learn more about it. Thank you again for letting me go to Skylan's competition. My offer still stands on helping you. If you ever need help mowing the lawn or anything. There is no need to pay me or anything, I am always happy to help you. Thank you for asking about how I am doing. I am doing great. School is going good. I didn't know if you wanted to know about my family or brother. My parents and I have gotten closer. My brother went to rehab, I am not sure if it will work but hopefully this time it will. I left a check inside for 1,000 dollars. If you want, I can send you a check to pay for her gymnastics fees.

February 13, 2009

Letter XVI

Steele Everest

P.S. If you ever decide you want to email me or call me. My email is <u>steeledog4@hotmail.com</u> *or my cell phone number is 555-456-4569*

I jumped out of bed then walked downstairs to the living room. Grandma Maggie was sitting on the couch. I sat down right beside her and looked right at her.

"I sort of understand why you kept it from me but then I wish you would have given me the opportunity to read the letters. I don't know if you made the right decision. I am guessing it was hard for you to tell me everything" I said

"I wanted to tell you but there hasn't been a perfect time to tell you. It was hard to tell you" Grandma Maggie said

"You could have told me when you asked for me a job at Steele's company." I said

"You are right but we have been fighting so much lately that I didn't know how to tell you. I needed you to start a job. I was sick of you laying around the house being depressed." Grandma Maggie said

Dang a little harsh Grandma Maggie

"I'm not arguing with you. I am going to talk to Steele about all the letters later. I need some fresh air." I said

"Okay, will I see you later?" Grandma Maggie said

"I don't know" I said

I walked back up the stairs to my room. I grabbed my purse, phone and letters. I walked back downstairs, right before I walked out the door. I told my Grandma Maggie that I loved her.

I walked to my car. Opened the door and hopped in the driver's seat. I turned the car on but I just sat there. I laid my head back and closed my eyes. So much had happened in the past 48 hours that I just needed a breather. My phone chimed. I picked it up to look at it.

"Hello Miss Mills, when do you think you will be here? Are we not having that business meeting anymore?" Steele texted

I had forgotten all about the business meeting. I became wrapped up in reading those letters. It had completely slipped my mind.

"We are going to need to postpone the meeting until tomorrow. I'm sorry for the inconvenience. We need to talk about the letters." I texted Steele

I wondered if Steele still had his letters from my Grandma Maggie then I wondered if the letters were as intense as the ones that Steele had given her.

"We really need to meet before this meeting. Since my Grandma Maggie showed me your letters you have sent over the years, I need to talk to you. Do you have your letters from her?" I texted Steele

"I do have them. Do I need to run home and go grab them? Do you want to meet me at my house? I kept them all." Steele immediately texted back.

"I will just meet you at your house. I want to talk but I really would like to read those letters. Honestly, can we postpone the meeting until next week? This is all so much for me to process in just the past couple of days." I texted

"Whatever you would like to do. I will agree to anything. I am truly sorry that I hurt you. I didn't want to lie to you. I hope one day you will forgive me. I will call the lawyers. Do you know what time next week so I can tell the lawyers?" Steele texted

FORGIVE HIM? LIARS. BOTH OF THEM. BOTH OF THE PEOPLE I LOVED.

I couldn't believe anything that happened. Steele and my Grandma Maggie lied to me for years. It was the only thought I could think of at the moment. I had fallen in love with Steele. The only family I had left was my Grandma Maggie. Two of the people that I loved in my life were now gone. Both of them were liars, I didn't know how to forgive them. I understand they thought they were making the correct decision at the time but it wasn't right to me. It was crazy to me.

I didn't know how to go on from that moment. The last two people I loved on the planet. Even though I was calm about it with my Grandma Maggie it was still something that I couldn't fully deal with.

"No, I have no idea currently. I just know that I would really like to read the letters you have from my Grandma Maggie." I texted back

"Okay, that is fine. I will meet you at my house." Steele text

I pulled up to Steele's house. I saw that Steele had already beat me there. He walked outside to meet me.

"I need to tell you something, you might be mad. Just promise me that you won't do anything stupid" Steele said

What could be so serious that he would tell me that? Why couldn't I just read the letters that my Grandma Maggie sent him?

"My brother Mac, found the letters. Mac burned all of them. I don't know why Mac did it. Mac is drunk so Mac won't tell me. He is in the living room watching TV now. You don't have to come in if you don't want to but I wanted to inform you that he was here. I wish I could have given you those letters before he found them. I should have scanned them and kept a copy. This is all my fault. I am extremely sorry." Steele said with tears in his eyes.

I was extremely disappointed that I didn't know what to do at that moment. Should I leave or walk in? The letters were turned to ash so I couldn't read them.

"All the letters are gone? Not one is left?" I asked for confirmation.

"Yes, all the letters were burned. I don't know how my brother found them but he did. He took all the letters. There wasn't one left. I wish you could have read those letters." Steele said

"I think I am going to go" I said

"Hold on please. I didn't think Mac would be here. I thought that Mac was with my parents. I knew you wouldn't want to see him so I thought my parents came to pick him up. I know this isn't what you were expecting. It's not the idea I had planned out in my head either. I understand you want to leave. Just text me when you are ready to meet with the lawyers. I understand you have been informed of an abundance of history the past few days. I will wait for a text or a call when you want to meet with the lawyers." Steele said

"I just really wanted to read those letters. There isn't anywhere that you scanned and saved copies?" I asked

"No, I never thought that I would need to. The letters were in my safe, I never thought that my brother would be in there. Never would I have thought that Mac would burn them." Steele said

"I will text or email you when I am ready. Thank you very much." I said

"You're very welcome." Steele said as he grinned.

"Bye" I said as I rolled my eyes.

His brother burned the letters. His brother had barely been out of rehab for a month. Mac already ruined my life with his existence. I just wished Mac would have fallen over and died. I knew I shouldn't have thought Steele should be dead but he killed my parents. Just to add to the pain Mac burned the letters as soon as I found out about them. I couldn't believe Steele's brother decided it was a good idea to burn the letters. I wasn't even able to read one of the letters. I just wanted to read them at least once.

I cried as I walked back to my car. I wanted to be mad at Steele for everything. It was his fault, I just couldn't stay mad at him. No matter what, I had fallen in love with Steele. I tried to see that after everything that Steele did for me, he still tried to do right by me. Steele didn't have to send my Grandma Maggie money every month like he was paying child support. Steele didn't need to give me a job or go to my graduations. Steele didn't need to go to any of my meets or school events but he did. Steele never bragged about it to me.

Steele never said anything about spending most of his time on me. I wondered how Steele didn't resent me for every moment that he didn't live to the fullest because he watched me grow up. All the time Steele took to write all the letters he sent. He wrote those letters with such care and consideration. Steele was such a humble and kind person.

Of course a few minutes later I received a text from Steele.

"I am sorry about everything that happened. I promise none of this was planned. The last action I wanted to take is to make you angrier at me." Steele texted

But it was too late for me to get madder at him. I had tear after tear roll down my cheeks. Nothing could stop those raindrops from pouring from my eyes. I was thankful that Steele didn't call me because I wouldn't have been able to pick up the phone while holding it together.

"I just need some time to think. I was really determined to read those letters. If you do end up finding extra copies to the letters that my Grandma Maggie wrote. Please call or text me." I texted

"I am in a meeting right now but I will call you after, I promise and if you need anything. Don't hesitate to call or text me." Steele texted

"I wish life was different. I wish that you and my Grandma Maggie would have told me the truth sooner. I hate that you or her couldn't tell me. You watched me grow up, you were there for everything. Why should I let you be part of my life now?" I texted Steele

"I am sorry that your life turned out differently than you imagined but your Grandma Maggie was only doing what she thought was best for you at the time. I respected her wishes because I thought she knew best. I can't change the past or know what it would have been like if you and I had grown up both knowing each other. All I can do is try to be there for you as much as I can from now on." Steele texted

"I just need some time to think. I will get back with you soon." I texted

145

"I will give you all the time you need. I just hope you aren't mad at me or your Grandma Maggie forever. Especially your Grandma Maggie. She loves you so much. Would you still like me to give you a call after this meeting?" Steele texted

Instead of texting him back right away, I read more letters.

Hello Mrs. Maggie Mills,

I went to more of her meets again. She is very talented. I am glad that you and she are doing well. My brother is doing good in rehab as of right now. My business is succeeding. This is going to be my last semester in school. I decided to put more into my business than in school. My parents aren't for it but I told them it's my decision. I left a check for 1,100 dollars. I hope the extra 100 dollars will cover her gymnastic fees. If not then I will send more. Thank you for taking the time to write to me and read my letters.

March 15, 2009

Letter XVII

Steele Everest

P.S. If you ever decide you want to email me or call me. My email is steeledog4@hotmail.com *or my cell phone number is 555-456-4569*

After I read multiple letters of what Steele had written to my Grandma Maggie, I was confused. I could hear the words from the letters coming from his mouth. It was like Steele hadn't changed since he started writing the letters. Other than the biggest secret of my life, Steele showed me kindness and candor every day I went into work. I had a crush on that man for as long as I could remember. I fell in love with that man in the short time I worked for him. I had seen Steele at my meets but I never knew who he was there for.

Hello Mrs. Maggie Mills,

I realize it's been a while since I wrote to you. I had some family problems come up, I hope you are still getting the checks that I have been sending you. My business is still going good as of right now. I hope you and Skylan are doing well.

September 15, 2009

Letter XVIII

Steele Everest

P.S. If you ever decide you want to email me or call me. My email is steeledog4@hotmail.com or my cell phone number is 555-456-4569

I drove all the way back to my Grandma Maggie's. I went straight to my room then started reading more letters. There were so many letters, I needed to read them all.

Hello Mrs. Maggie Mills,

Merry Christmas to you and Skylan. I hope you are both doing well. I received your letter with Skylan's gymnastic schedule. Thank you very much for that. I plan on going to all of them. I have been busy but I still haven't missed a meet yet. I left a 1,000 dollar check in envelope. Let me know if you need more. My family is doing great. Thank you for asking about them.

December 15, 2009

Letter XIX

Steele Everest

P.S. If you ever decide you want to email me or call me. My email is steeledog4@hotmail.com or my cell phone number is 555-456-4569

After reading the letters I started to realize that Steele had done a tremendous job over the years with giving my Grandma Maggie money and support. Steele never had to support us even after all those years. I accepted that I couldn't blame him for the accident. I still wasn't ready to forgive his brother, but I could forgive him. I decided to text him, and I was finally ready to meet with the lawyers.

"No, I don't want you to call me. All the information can be translated over text. Tomorrow at 9 AM. I am ready to meet with the lawyers. Thank you very much for the time you put into going to my events. Thank you for all the support you had given to my Grandma Maggie and me over the years. Thank you for still writing letters to my Grandma Maggie." I texted Steele back

I was still in so much pain but I knew I would need more than a week to heal from all the lies and secrets my Grandma Maggie and Steele put me through. I knew they did it out of love but it still didn't make it hurt any less. My love for Steele only grew stronger after reading all of the letters he sent. I knew that my feelings for him were not going away any time soon. Steele was almost perfect. I decided to read one letter before bed, each night. There were too many letters for me to read with all the emotions I felt with each letter.

I knew what I wanted from Steele. I knew that Steele would give me anything I asked from him. I heard my phone ding. I quickly picked up my phone to look at the message.

"You are very welcome. I will cancel all my plans in the morning. Having the meeting in my office okay with you?" Steele texted

"Yes, that is fine. I will see you tomorrow" I texted Steele back

20

TWENTY letters later...

I decided to read one more letter then I would go to sleep. That next morning was going to be one of the biggest mornings of my life. I picked up the last letter for the day then went into focus.

Hello Mrs. Maggie Mills,

I hope that you had a great Christmas. I hope this year has been good so far. I hope that it's better than last year. Thank you for responding to my letters. I understand that I haven't been as responsive as I have been in the past. I have really been trying to stay busy and keep my business going as well as still going to Skylan's meets. She is really good. I know people usually drop out of it but she should really keep up the good work. I left a 1,000 dollar check in the envelope. I hope y'all have a good Valentine's Day.

February 9, 2010

Letter XX

Steele Everest

P.S. If you ever decide you want to email me or call me. My email is steeledog4@hotmail.com or my cell phone number is 555-456-4569

Since I had the biggest meeting of my life the next day, I didn't want to go to bed. My anxiety was so bad but I knew I needed some sleep.

"Raya, set my alarm for 6AM" I said

I slept quite well that night.

"The sun is shining, birds are chirping, it is beautiful outside. Wakey wakey." my alarm clock, Raya said

I crawled out of bed then I walked into my bathroom. Just like any other day, I stripped my clothes then I hopped in the shower, I felt the hot water glide down my body. I stood there for a little while before I reached for the soap. I thought about what was going to happen that day. I knew my life was about to change forever. I knew that I couldn't go back after what I decided to do.

I reached for my face wash, put a little on my fingers then rotated in circular motions on my face while I thought about Steele's huge heart. Would everything I was asking for change his feelings for me? Would he hate me after today? So many questions were unanswered before this meeting.

I stood under the water while the soap from my face cleared off. I grabbed the shampoo, put a little in my hand and lathered the soap into my hair. I scrubbed my scalp for a few seconds then put my body under the shower. I ran my fingers through my hair to rinse all the shampoo out. I picked up the conditioner then put some conditioner in my hand. I was extremely stressed to the point my hair was falling out as if I was taking chemotherapy. I reached for the body wash, put a little on my hand. As I washed my body, I started to think about what exactly I would tell Steele when I saw him. Then I thought to myself. Would I see him before the meeting or after the meeting? Would I see him alone ever again? If I do see him at any point by myself should I even talk to him?

"CRAP!" I yelled

I thought in my head, I hope I don't need a lawyer for this meeting. I didn't know if I should trust Steele

I washed the soap off, I just stood under the hot running water. It felt refreshing, but I knew I was about to step out. I turned the water off then stepped out of the shower. I grabbed my towel that hung from the towel rack to dry off. I dried my whole body then bent over and wrapped my hair in my towel. I grabbed a robe from the hook that was screwed to the wall. I brushed my teeth slowly. I finished brushing my teeth. Then unwrapped my towel from my hair. I brushed through my hair with my wet brush. I put some product in my hair. I washed my hands then walked into my room.

I looked at my phone, I had a text message from Steele. I opened it immediately.

"We are still having this meeting at 9AM, correct?" Steele's text messaged stated

"Yes, we are" I replied

I sat my phone on the bed. I walked over to my vanity. I started putting makeup on, I always felt a little better after I put makeup on. I sat there staring at myself in the mirror. I drew a blank to every thought I had that morning. I closed my eyes and took a deep breath. I opened my eyes, stood up, and walked into my closet. I picked out an outfit that I thought would go good with my meeting. It was a black pencil skirt with a belt with a peplum top that was solid white. Since I was wearing a pencil skirt, I decided to wear pencil heel shoes.

I grabbed my phone, threw it in my purse, grabbed the keys then headed downstairs. It was 7:30AM when I was walking out the door. I wasn't sure where my Grandma Maggie was at but I wasn't too concerned. I unlocked the door to my new car. I stepped in, threw my purse in the passenger seat. I went straight to Steele's company. I turned on the radio to create noise. The traffic was terrible that day. It took me the full hour and a half I spared myself to arrive at the building. That didn't count the moments it took to park then walk up to the office.

I went straight to the 25th floor, right before I arrived at the 25 floor, my phone started to ring. It was the therapist's office. OMG. I completely forgot about my therapist appointment.

"Hello" I answered the phone

"Hello, is this Miss Mills?" the receptionist said

"Yes, it is" I said

"You missed your appointment, do you want to reschedule?" the receptionist said

"Yes, I would like to do that" I said

"Okay, when is a good time for you" the receptionist said

"Next Tuesday okay?" I asked

"Okay, morning or afternoon" the receptionist said

"Morning" I said

"Is 11 o'clock in the morning okay?"

"Yes that is fine" I said

"Okay see you then" the receptionist said

I walked into Steele's office. He was waiting for me with three other people at his long business table.

"Good morning, Miss Mills" the accountant said as he shook my hand

"Good morning, Miss Mills" the lawyer said as he shook my hand

"Good morning Miss Mills" Steele said as he tried to give me a hug

"Good morning, everyone" I said

We all sat down at the big conference table, I was so nervous that it felt like my heart was about to pop out of my chest.

"I have filled everyone in on what is going on so we don't have to explain. Would you like the money sent to your checking account and how much do you want?" Steele said

"I want you to pay for the house. I want 1,500 dollars sent to my account each week. Also I want to keep my job, if that is okay with you Steele." I demanded

"Do you have all your account information to send it as a direct deposit?" The accountant said

"Yes, I do. Here is a check so you have my account number and my routing number." I said as I handed the check to the accountant.

"All sounds good to me. The lawyers will draw up the paperwork. Then we will have another meeting to make sure the paperwork is good with you. I am happy that you want to keep your job" Steele said

"Thank you. I am still in the process of reading all the letters. Thank you for accepting my requests" I said

I didn't want to call the requests, demands. I figured that would be rude or disrespectful. Steele might have lied to me but he had been the nicest person I had ever met too.

I walked out of the room. I was about to walk into the elevator when Steele yelled my name. He was running out of his office.

"Skylan! Can we have dinner tonight?" Steele asked with excitement

I didn't know what to say because I was sure that Steele just asked me out on a date

"Like a date?" I asked

"I would like it to be but it doesn't have to be a date. It can be two people just having dinner together." Steele said

"What time?" I asked

"Is six o'clock okay with you?" Steele asked

"Yes, that sounds fine. What should I wear?" I asked

I knew going on a date with Steele would be different than going on a date with anyone else.

"Whatever you would like to wear" Steele said

"Where are we going to dinner" I asked

"It's a surprise, you can wear anything. Wear something comfortable. We aren't going to a place with a dress code." Steele said

Comfortable. Could Steele be any more of a guy?

"Okay, I will see you at 6 o'clock" I said

"Okay see you then" Steele said

I decided to grab something to eat before I went home. I was nervous so I knew I wouldn't be able to eat something big. I rode the elevator all the way down to the parking garage. The meeting went by faster than I anticipated. I went directly to my car. I was a little nervous because of the accident with his brother in the parking garage. I jumped in my car. Immediately locked my doors. I put my purse in the passenger seat. My phone connected to my radio then started playing music. First song that came on was "Good Day by Nappy Roots." I put my seatbelt on then headed out of the parking garage. It was a relief to drive out of the parking garage without getting hurt. I decided to make it cheap and quick. I saw a McDonald's so I pulled into the drive through. I ordered a McChicken, a small fry and a Dr. Pepper. I drove to the first window, I handed the woman my card. The employee handed me back my card and a receipt. I drove to the second window for the employee to hand me my food. I was ready to be home. More than likely I would be going to work tomorrow plus I had a date tonight with my boss who happened to be much more than my boss. I figured when I arrived home, that I would just read some more letters. I didn't have anything else better to do. I wasn't going to start getting ready for my date with my boss right away. On my way home, I decided to set it on cruise. I ate my McChicken and my fries on my way home. It didn't take as long getting home as it did driving to Everest Corp. I pulled into the garage, I stepped out of the car. My Grandma Maggie was home but she was asleep. I didn't wake her, I just went straight to my room. I wanted to be comfortable so I changed out of my clothes that I wore to the business meeting. I put a comfy t-shirt on then crawled into bed. I turned on the television. I decided to read one letter then go back to sleep since I didn't have anything to do for hours.

Hello Mrs. Maggie Mills,

You should be extremely proud of yourself for Skylan. I hope that she is doing better. She seems to look happier. You are so blessed to have a granddaughter with such amazing talent. I hope both of you had a great Valentine's Day. I will be at Skylan's competition this weekend. Have a great week. I wrote a 1,000 dollar check for Skylan's account.

February 22, 2010

Letter XXI

Steele Everest

P.S. If you ever decide you want to email me or call me. My email is steeledog4@hotmail.com or my cell phone number is 555-456-4569

I put the letter with the rest of the letters that I had read. It made my heart so happy because Steele never stopped caring about me.

"Raya set an alarm for 4:30 o'clock" I said to my alarm

"Alarm set for 4:30 o'clock in the afternoon" my alarm Raya said

"The sun is shining, the earth is spinning, and you are wonderful. It's time to jump out of bed" My alarm clock Raya said

I didn't want to wake up, much less jump out of bed. I just wanted to sleep the day away. I decided to roll out of bed. I walked to my closet, I stood there staring at my clothes. I didn't have any type of clothes to wear on a date with Steele. I figured we would go to an expensive, over the top place. I chose to put on a fancy sundress. I hoped that the sundress would be good enough for the restaurant Steele picked. I chose sandals instead of fancy heels to match my sundress

I sat down at my makeup vanity. I put a headband on my head to pull my hair out of the way of my face. I padded my foundation then applied my blush. I put mascara on, which always took the longest. I looked at the clock. It was 5:45 PM. Steele was always right on time so I knew he would be at my house in 15 minutes. I put my matte pink lipstick on. I switched purses to match my outfit. I had noticed it was one minute before 6PM so I started walking downstairs. Steele had walked up to the door and knocked on the door. I was so nervous, I didn't know what to think. I was probably going to end up stuttering.

I walked to the front door and opened it.

"Wow, you look incredible!" Steele said

"You don't look so bad yourself" I said

Steele was drop dead gorgeous

Steele wore a flower printed short sleeve collar shirt with plain yellow beach shorts. He had fixed his hair with gel that made him look even sexier. There was no way I could ever out dress this guy.

"Where are we going?" I asked

"I was thinking this good restaurant on the beach" Steele said

"Which beach?" I asked

"South Padre Island, there is this place called the Sea Ranch. I love it! After we are done eating we can walk on the beach. Is that okay with you?" Steele said

"I guess we are going in your helicopter?" I asked

"Yes, you are correct. It would take too long to drive down there." Steele said

It all seemed like a dream that I was soon going to wake up from. I couldn't believe everything that happened. It was so sweet, he was so sweet. I figured people would start taking pictures of us and start talking about us. I wasn't some assistant that jumped in bed with my boss so I wasn't sure if he was okay with being seen in public with me. Steele watched me grow up from the time I was ten years old.

I was so excited about flying in the helicopter again. Steele of course

156

opened the door for me to step into the car. I didn't think I would ever become tired of him being such a gentleman.

As soon as we were both in the car, Steele started talking

"So I know that I have watched you grow up but I want to get to know the real you. I only know what your Grandma Maggie has told me. You were practically a stranger to me until you stepped into my office your first day of work. I want to know all of you, if that is okay with you?" Steele said

I honestly was going to pass out after Steele told me that he wanted to know the real me.

"I have been lost recently, I am trying to figure out who I am without school and gymnastics. My whole life has been planned. After gymnastics stopped in high school I still had school but that went away after college. I always had something going on in my life. I didn't exactly know what to do a few months ago when everything stopped. I am just trying to figure out who I am right now" I said

"I understand. I don't know who I would be if I didn't have my company and you in my life. For so long my attention has been you and my company. Now that I am getting to actually know you, I don't think I could lose you now. I want to give you the whole world." Steele said

How could I be mad at someone who wants to give me the whole world? It's almost like nothing mattered but me. I wasn't sure if it was good or bad that Steele felt lost without me.

"You have given me everything I have asked for and more. You make my life seem more of a dream than reality. I don't know if I will completely move on from the fact that you have been part of my life since I was 10. You have been there for over a decade, cheering me on. It's hard to not give you a chance." I said

I was so in love with Steele that the love gave me butterflies in my stomach every time I saw him. Steele was charming, genuine, loving, kind, caring, amazing, attractive, sexy, smart...oh, I could go on and on.

157

"I don't want you to feel obligated to be around me" Steele said

Steele had to be kidding. He was everything any girl would want. I was complicated and not together in many different ways. How does Steele not see that I am in love with him? Even after everything that he lied about, I am still here giving him a chance.

"I want to be here with you" I said

We arrived at the helicopter pad.

"It's approximately an hour flight. I hope you love seafood. I forgot to ask" Steele said

"You're good. I love seafood." I said

Even though so much had happened, I could still see myself spending the rest of my life with this romantic, caring and sweet man. Steele was so close to perfect.

"Have you ever eaten at Seafood Ranch before?" Steele said

"Umm no I have not, I am excited to try it" I said

I knew that I would more than likely love anything I had from there. I was so grateful to have this man in my life. I knew there wasn't a perfect person on this planet so it's the reason I forgave him for hiding that he was there my whole life. I forgave him for not keeping the keys from his brother but he didn't kill my parents.

The flight went extremely fast, we were at Brownsville in no time. He had a car waiting for us to take us to the restaurant. The driver opened the door for me from the helicopter and the car Steele had waiting for us. It was incredible.

Once we were in the car, not much was said. I enjoyed the view headed to South Padre. When we arrived at the restaurant, the driver opened up the door for me. I loved everything about the date, it was almost too good to be true.

"Are you ready to go inside?" Steele asked

"Absolutely" I said

When we walked inside the restaurant, the person at the door greeted us right away. I guess Steele had already made reservations because we were seated right away.

Steele pulled out my chair. As I sat down in my chair, I looked up at him. The chemistry that I felt between us two in the moment was a connection I knew that no one could break. Steele then pushed my chair closer to the table. Then Steele sat down, we both started to look at the menu that the greeter had handed us.

I had no clue what to order. I was so nervous I felt as though my organs were going to fall out of my butt.

Our waiter came up to our table

"What would you like to drink?" the waiter said

"I will take some water, please" I said

Even though I needed a liquid that could have been a little bit stronger

"I will take a water as well, thank you" Steele said

"Two waters coming up" the waiter said

"I am going to need a minute to look at this menu because I have no clue what I am going to order" I said

"Take all the time you need" Steele said

"Do you know what you are going to order?" I asked

"I have an idea" Steele said

The waiter came back to the table

"Here are your waters. Are you ready to order yet? Would you like an appetizer?" the waiter said

"Do you want the Mussels?" Steele asked me

"I am okay with that" I said

I went back to looking at the menu. I knew that Steele was staring at me. I wanted to smile so big because I could feel what he was feeling. We were in complete sync with each other. After all these years, we were finally together.

It was amazing. I knew that Steele was the one. He was going to be the one forever. I felt the love with every bone in my body. It scared me because Steele had been there for me even when I didn't know he was there, all without credit. Steele risked everything over the years for me.

"Okay, I will let the kitchen know about those mussels. Do you need more time for the entree?" the waiter asked

"Are you ready?" Steele asked

I flew back to Earth

"Yes, I think I am ready" I said

Even though I didn't really know what I wanted.

"I guess I will take the Red Snapper, blackened and I would like the filet with scalloped potatoes and a salad with Ranch please" I said

"And you sir?" the waiter asked

"I am going to take Tyler's Tuna, blackened please. I would like a salad with Ranch and sweet potato fries" Steele said

"Okay, I will put your order in. Is there anything else I can bring you?" the waiter said

"No thank you" I said

"We are good for now thank you" Steele said

The waiter brought us the mussels and our salads.

"This is really good. Thank you for bringing me here" I said

"Oh course. Anytime" Steele said

The waiter brought us our entree. It looked so good. I was ready to dig in, however I looked up at Steele

"Would you like to pray with me?" Steele asked

"I would love to pray with you" I said

"Good" Steele said

We bowed our heads then he led us in prayer.

"Dear Heavenly Father, thank you for all the blessings you have given Skylan and me today. Bless this food with the nourishment to our bodies. Forgive us for the sins that we have committed. Keep Skylan and me safe on our way back home please in Jesus Name Amen" Steele said

It had been a while since I had prayed before I ate dinner. It was nice to pray at the table. Before my parents died I always prayed at the table. When I moved into my Grandma Maggie's house we did pray at the beginning but then I started eating in my room and I quit praying. It wasn't the same after my parents died. I wanted to tell Steele all of that but we were having such a good time.

Steele paid for our food then we walked out of the restaurant.

"Do you want to go walk on the beach for a few minutes before we have to head back?" Steele asked

"Absolutely, I would love to do that" I said

We both jumped in the car, the driver took us to a beach that he drove out on.

"Do you want to take your shoes off? I'm going to take mine off" Steele asked

"Yes, I do" I said

We both took our shoes off

"Let me open the door please" Steele said

"Okay" I said

Steele jumped out then ran over to the other side of the car

"Here you go" Steele said

"Thank you very much" I said

"You're welcome" Steele said

I was just breathing in the amazing date I was on. We watched the sunset while we walked on the beach.

We drew our names in the sand. Before the water washed it away, we took a picture. It was cheesy and cliché but I didn't care because I was in love with Steele. Everything felt perfect. The first time in a very long time, everything was perfect.

"Skylan" Steele said

"Yes" I said

I looked up at him as he looked down at me. Steele took each one of his hands, placed them within mine. His fingers intertwined with mine. He fixated his beautiful eyes on me. It was though time stood still. My heart was pumping so fast and hard that I was afraid he could hear it. There were a million butterflies in my stomach. I had chill bumps from the top of my head to the bottom of my feet. My legs were so weak I thought I might fall standing there.

Steele tilted his head down, our eyes closed. Our mouths opened and closed slowly. It felt like electricity going through my whole body. It was a kiss like nothing before. We were completely connected in those few seconds. I wanted to keep going but I didn't want to move quicker than I was comfortable with.

"I don't want to go too fast" I said as I gently pushed away and looked down.

Steele took his hand to my chin then lifted my head up

"I'm okay with going slow, as long as you know that I love you. I am madly in love with you" Steele said

I stood there for a moment breathing in the fact that Steele just told me that he loved me. I couldn't believe it.

"I'm happy that you are okay with that, I love you too" I said

It was incredible. We walked back to the car. I wiped the sand off of me then jumped in the car.

The rest of the way home I floated on a cloud. It was like it was all a dream. My heart was happier than it had been in years.

Once I arrived home, I looked at my phone. I was planning on texting Steele but my phone had multiple notifications. One of them was a voicemail from one of my Grandma Maggie's friends.

"Sweetie this is Ethel, I need you to meet me at the hospital. It is very important. Your Grandma Maggie is here." the voicemail from Ethel said

I immediately called her back

"What is going on? I need to know what is happening. What is wrong with my Grandma Maggie? Is she okay?" I said

"Can you please just come to the hospital? Be careful driving please" Ethel said

"Yes, I will be there shortly" I said

I hurried to my room to change clothes. I was crying because I wasn't sure what was going on. My Grandma Maggie had never been in the hospital before.

I ran and jumped in my car. I drove straight to the hospital. Once I arrived at the hospital, I threw my mask on then headed into the waiting room. I immediately saw my Grandma Maggie's friend Ethel.

"We are having to wait out here in the waiting room. I haven't heard anything about her. I came to the house to check on her. Your grandma wasn't answering the phone, which isn't like her. I tried to call you but you weren't answering either. I drove to your house, no one answered the door so I walked inside. Luckily, the door was unlocked. Your grandma was unconscious so I immediately called 911. The ambulance brought her to the hospital, I haven't heard from anyone since I arrived" Ethel said

"Family of Maggie Mills?" a doctor called out into the waiting room.

"Yes, that is me. I am her granddaughter" I said

"Okay, your grandmother had a heart attack. We tried everything we could but she didn't make it. I am sorry" the doctor said

"I am sorry, she what? There is no way. She was fine" I said

"I am sorry, would you like to see her" the doctor said

"Yes, I would like to see her" I said

I walked back to a room. It was like tunnel vision. I couldn't see anything but the doctor leading me to the room

I sat down beside her bed, then laid my head on her body. I sat there. I couldn't say any words.

I was completely alone. I didn't know what to do. The first person who popped in my mind was Steele. I called him. Steele quickly answered.

"Hello, Miss Mills. I just made it home. I was about to text you. I wasn't sure if you were still awake." Steele said

"My Grandma Maggie is dead." I said

"Where are you?" Steele said

"I'm at the hospital" I said

"Don't leave. I will be right there" Steele said

"Okay" I said

I hung up. I was crying so hard I didn't know what to do. My Grandma Maggie was all I had left. Steele showed up and immediately hugged me.

"I am so sorry for your loss. If it is okay with you, I am going to take care of everything for you." Steele said

Steele stuck with his word, he took care of everything. My Grandma Maggie had a will set up, so most of it was laid out. The whole week was mostly a blur. I don't remember much but Steele was perfect about everything. He had taken care of the cost that the life insurance didn't cover. Steele was too kind about everything. For about a week after the funeral I laid in bed. Everyday Steele or someone called me. I just ignored all of the calls and messages.

One day, Steele walked into my bedroom then turned the lights on.

The lights hurt my eyes so much that I covered my head with my blanket

"Skylan, you have to wake up. You need to take a shower and eat something. I am concerned about you" Steele said

I laid there. I couldn't say anything. Steele slowly walked to my bed.

"I think if you take a shower you will feel a little better." Steele said

I didn't move or make a sound.

"I am going to pick you up to take you to the shower. Is that okay?" Steele asked

I didn't make any movements. I didn't make any sounds. I was so weak there was no way I could stand.

"Skylan, is that okay?" Steele asked

I uncovered my face

"Yes" I said with a light scratchy voice.

"Okay. I will have everything ready for you in the bathroom" Steele said

Steele shortly came back. He picked me up then took me straight to the bathtub. Steele had already put soap and water in the bathtub.

My body was so extremely weak that when he sat me down, my head went back and my eyes closed. My legs fell straight to the tub. My arms laid beside my body.

"I am going to scrub your body with this loofa." Steele said

He did exactly that

"Do you want to wash your private areas?" Steele asked

"I can do that?" I said very quietly.

Steele gently handed me the loofa.

I washed myself then handed him back the loofa.

"I am going to wash your hair now" Steele said

Steele squirted a small amount of shampoo in his palm then gently washed my hair. After, he grabbed the shower head then washed all the soap out of my hair.

"I am now going to put conditioner on your hair" Steele said

"Okay" I said

Steele put conditioner on my hair. Steele scrubbed my hair then washed the shampoo out. He drained the water then sprayed all the soap off of me. Steele had grabbed a towel in the cabinet. He picked me up with the towel then carried me to my bedroom. He laid me on my bed then grabbed some clothes.

"Do you want to put these on or do I need to put them on for you?" Steele asked

"I can put them on" I said

Steele had picked out leggings and a t-shirt with a sports bra and underwear.

"I am going to go downstairs and see if there is anything I can cook for you. If you would like you can come down after you put some clothes on" Steele said

"I will come down after I put some clothes on" I said

"Okay good" Steele said

I couldn't believe he had given me a bath. It was embarrassing but there was no way I would have done it. I put my clothes on then walked downstairs

"I am sorry to tell you but you have no food for me to fix. Do you want me to send Mr. Busch to grab us some food" Steele said

"I probably need to step out of this house. So can we go grab something to eat? I don't want to go anywhere fancy." I said

"Of course we can. It doesn't have to be fancy. Do you have something in mind?" Steele asked

"No" I said

"Okay, I will figure it out." Steele said

We both walked out to his car. I was so weak when I climbed in the backseat. If Steele wouldn't have helped me then I wouldn't have been able to crawl into the car.

We drove all the way into Austin. I barely remembered the drive. I didn't say anything the whole way there. It took us about forty-five minutes but we finally arrived at his house. I was confused because I figured we were headed to a restaurant.

"I thought we were going to a restaurant" I said

"I decided to cook you something at my house. I am glad you left the house but I figured you wouldn't want to be around a bunch of people." Steele said

He was correct. I knew I needed to leave the house. Plus I did needed to eat. I just didn't want to be around people.

"Thank you" I said

"You are more than welcome. Can you walk into the house or do I need to help you?" Steele said

"I think I can make it" I said

I walked halfway to the front door then almost fell. Steele had swept me up before I fell completely to the ground. He carried me straight to the couch.

Steele made grilled chicken, sweet potatoes and broccoli. He also made some caramelized carrots that I was ready to try. It wasn't anything fancy but it was food that Steele made himself.

"I can make your plate. Do you want everything on it?" Steele asked

"Yes, please" I said

"Okay" Steele said

Steele put a little bit of everything on my plate.

"Thank you" I said

I decided to wait to eat until his plate was ready.

"Do you mind if I say a prayer out loud?" Steele said

"I absolutely do not mind at all" I said

We both bowed our heads and closed our eyes.

"Dear Heavenly Father, bless this food in front of us with the nourishment of our bodies. Thank you for allowing Skylan and I to come together. Please help Skylan feel better and help her in the process of the loss of her grandmother. Forgive our sins that we have committed. Thank you for this day that you have given us. In Jesus name, Amen" Steele prayed

"Amen" I said

I haven't prayed with anyone at the table besides my parents and my Grandma Maggie. Praying with him was different than praying with my parents or grandma. Unfortunately, I couldn't eat all my food. I ate everything that I could eat, I just couldn't eat it all.

"Would you like to stay here? I have an extra bedroom?" Steele said

"Yeah, if that is okay. Can we stay up just a little longer? Maybe watch TV." I said

"That sounds perfect" Steele said

We walked into the TV room. Steele turned on the television. I honestly didn't know what we were watching. I fell asleep on Steele five minutes into the movie.

I woke up in a strange room. It had cream walls with all matching furniture. The bed was the most comfortable bed I had ever slept on. The sheets were so soft, I honestly could have slept all day in that bed. I looked at the clock that was on the nightstand.

"OMG, IT'S 2 IN THE AFTERNOON!" I yelled

I jumped out of bed then I walked out of the beautiful, strange room. I walked to the kitchen where I saw Steele cooking us breakfast. Honestly should have been lunch since the day was half way over.

I sat down at the bar in his kitchen

"I figured I would sneak you into the office today. You don't have to do anything. If you don't want to go to the office then we can go to the park or we can stay here. Whatever you like to do today. Mr. Busch brought you some clothes from your house. He brought you work clothes and comfy clothes." Steele said

"Okay thank you. Can you go to the cemetery?" I asked

"Yes, if that is what you want to do. We can do that." Steele said

He put a plate of food in front of me.

"I hope you like it?" Steele said

"I probably will but I probably can't eat it all" I said

"Just eat what you can. I'm not going to kill you if you don't eat it all." Steele said

After I ate, I went back to that room. I put on some different comfortable clothes. I put my tennis shoes on then walked back to the kitchen. Steele was cleaning the kitchen.

"Are you ready to go?" Steele asked

"Yes I am, are you?" I asked

"Absolutely, let's go. Mr. Busch is out front in the car" Steele said

We walked out to the car. Nothing was said the whole car ride to the cemetery. He drove straight to my grandparent's grave, right next to their grave was my parents.

"I will give you a minute" Steele said

"Thank you" I said

I walked right to them. I didn't say anything. I just stood there and cried. Steele walked up to me a few minutes later, I leaned into his chest.

"I can't believe they are gone" I said

"I am sorry, I wish I could do more. Unfortunately, all the money in the world can't fix this problem. I know they are all in a better place." Steele said

"I know" I said

"Are you ready to go back to the car?" Steele asked

"Yes" I said

"Do you want to go for a drive or where would you like to go?" Steele asked as we walked back to the car

"Actually, can we go to the office? I don't want to do anything but I can sit in your office while you do some work. I know you have a bunch of work to do" I said

"If that is what you want to do, that is fine with me" Steele said

We stepped into the car. The ride to the office was quiet. Once we arrived, we went straight to his office. Steele must have said something to the employees because we made it all the way to his office without one person talking to me.

"If you want you can sit on the couch. I can turn the TV on if you want me to or I can give you a book" Steele said

"I would rather watch TV right now if you can work and let me watch TV" I said

"Of course I can" Steele said

Steele turned on the TV then gave me the remote control. I turned on a show that I had never watched before. I didn't pay attention to the show. I mostly just stared at the television while I thought about the fact that I had no family left.

The next couple months went similar to that day. Not much had changed in the day to day basics. One day I woke up in Steele's guest room. I walked into the kitchen. That day, I felt peace. It felt as though everything would be okay. I felt okay. After we ate breakfast, we went to the cemetery like we did for months, however this day was different.

Steele gave me some time alone with my parents and grandparents.

"I feel better today, I feel at peace. Steele has been the best support I could ever have asked for in my life. I am grateful that God put him in my life. I don't think I could have gotten through the past couple months without him. He has been my best friend, my angel and my heart. I thank God for him every day. I will see y'all tomorrow. I love all of you." I said at their graves

I walked back to the car, I jumped into the car.

"I feel good today. I think I am able to go back to my Grandma Maggie's house today" I said to Steele

"Okay, we will head that way" Steele said

I walked into my Grandma Maggie's house. I had mixed feelings about going in but I knew I needed to do it that day. I walked to her bedroom, everything was the same. I started packing everything up.

"I can have someone do this, you don't have to pack everything up." Steele said

"Yes, I do. I think I need to do this alone too. I will be okay, I will text you on the hour every hour. Do you want to go to work? Then come pick me up after you are off work? I would also like to go out to dinner with you tonight if that is okay?" I said

Steele walked over to me, he gave me a big hug.

"Of course, I will pick you up later. If you need anything then you can give me a call" Steele said

"Okay I will" I said

I kissed him. I hadn't kissed him since the night at the beach.

After he left, I started to pack up her clothes. I didn't pay attention to the time. I did it very slowly. Some clothes I would just hold in my arms and cry for a little bit. It was about noon. Steele walked up the stairs.

"I brought you some food. It's down there on the table. I figured you would still be busy packing. Do you want me to eat with you?" Steele said

"Yes please" I said

"Okay, good. I was hoping that you would want me to eat with you" Steele said

We walked down to the kitchen. We ate the food that he had brought.

"Thank you" I said

"You're welcome, anytime" Steele said

"No, thank you for everything that you have done in the past few months. Everything you have done from the time we met. You have gone beyond what anyone should ever do." I said

Steele kissed my forehead

"I am happy that you let me be there for you. It was the least I could do" Steele said

"You are too kind" I said

"Thank you for all your kind words" Steele said

I held his hand

"Of course" I said

"I am grateful that you are in my life" Steele said

"Me too. I am going to head back up to finish packing. Is there any way that you can start selling this furniture or do something with it? I want everything out of here but my bedroom." I said

"Yes, I can do that" Steele said

I didn't have much left to pack in my Grandma Maggie's room. Once I was all done, I walked downstairs to the kitchen. I started to pack up everything in the kitchen. I made a pile to keep and a pile to give away or sell.

I heard a knock on the door. I went straight to the door to see who it was. It was a few men with a moving van. They were there to help me with all the furniture and boxes. I guess Steele called a moving company right after he left.

"Can you start with the furniture then we can go from there?" I said

"Yes, ma'am" the men said

"Thank you" I said

I walked to my room while they were doing their job. I laid in my bed and cried. It was painful to pack all my Grandma Maggie's belongings but I knew I needed to do it. I heard someone knock on my bedroom door.

"Come in" I said

It was Steele.

"Hey, they are almost done with all the furniture. Do you still want to go eat?" Steele said

"Yes, I do. It doesn't need to be anywhere fancy." I said

"Okay, is Jim's Steakhouse okay with you?" Steele asked

"Not exactly what I was thinking but yes, we can go there" I said

"Okay, are you sure? I can pick something else" Steele said

"I am sure" I said

We walked to the car then we headed to the restaurant.

While we were in the car, I laid my head on him. We didn't say anything but he played with my hair and rubbed my back.

"We are here" Steele said

Steele had talked to Mr. Busch about making a reservation so we were seated right away.

"Hello, my name is Toni. I will be your waitress this evening. What drinks can I start you off with?" the waitress asked

"I want water" I said

"I want water as well" Steele said

"Okay two waters coming up" the waitress said

"I wanted to talk to you about our future" I said to Steele

"Yes" Steele said

"I was wondering if you wanted to move into my Grandma Maggie's house with me after everything is out of the house. We can make it ours. I can move into my Grandma Maggie's room and you can move into my room. Is that okay with you? I want to move back home but I want you to be there with me." I said

"Yes, I will" Steele said

"Are you sure? It's okay if you would like to think about it" I said

"Yes, I am sure. As long as I am with you, I don't care where we live" Steele said

"Here is water for you ma'am. Here is a water for you sir. Are y'all ready to order?" the waitress asked

"I am ready to order if she is ready to order" Steele said

"Yes, I am ready to order" I said

"I just want a 6 oz. steak, medium rare with green beans and a baked potato please. I want Ranch as my dressing for my salad" I said

"I want the 20 oz. ribeye. I want it cooked medium with a baked potato and caramelized carrots. I would also like Ranch on my salad" Steele said

"Okay, sounds good. I will have that out as soon as possible. Is there anything else I can get you?" the waitress said

"Yes, some rolls please" I said

"Yes, I am waiting for them in the oven. I will bring them out to you when the rolls are done." the waitress said

"Thank you" I said

The waitress walked away.

"I also would like to go back to therapy and work." I said

"Sounds like a perfect idea. Would you like to go back to the beach again?" Steele said

"Tonight?" I asked

"Yes, tonight" Steele said

"I guess we can go to the beach tonight" I said

"After we eat then we will head to the beach" Steele said

I wondered why he would want to go to the beach. Honestly I wanted to go home but he had helped me so much I couldn't say no to him.

"Here are your rolls. Would you like some more water?" the waitress

said

"Yes please" Steele and I both said at the same time

"Thanks" I said

"Thank you" Steele said

The waitress walked off for about 5 minutes then she came back with our food.

"Here you go ma'am" said the waitress while she handed me my food

"Here you go sir" said the waitress while she handed Steele his food

We ate our food then Steele paid.

"Are you ready to go to the beach" Steele asked

"Absolutely" I said

"Good" Steele said

We walked to the car while holding hands.

"Here you go Miss Mills" Steele said as he opened the door.

"Thank you" I said as I reached up and kissed him on the cheek.

"You're welcome" Steele said

We took the helicopter then jumped in a car.

Steele and I both took our shoes off then stepped out of the car. We walked out on the beach just like we did on our first official date. As soon as I stepped out on the beach there were lights hanging from poles formed in a square. There were rose petals in the shape of a heart. There were candles all around the outside of the rose petal heart. Directly in the middle of the rose petals there was a heart shaped sign that said MARRY ME PLEASE?

"Ummm Steele" I said

"I know it's been less than a year since we have really known each other but I fell in love with you from the moment I watched you work in your office on those invitations that I had you do. I didn't think I would ever find someone who I would want to spend the rest of my life with. Then I met you, I already knew that you had ambition. I knew you were independent and strong. I wasn't planning on falling in love with you when you came to work for me but I did. I don't regret one moment that we have spent together. I know that we aren't normal co-workers and friends but would you do me the honors and please marry me?" Steele said

"Steele. Are you sure?" I asked

Steele was kneeling on one knee with a ring that was huge and beautiful. It was a 3 carat yellow gold ring with a round cut. It had a big diamond in the middle with smaller diamonds around the big diamond. Then there were diamonds halfway down the side of the band.

"I have never been more sure of anything in my life" Steele said

"I need to go, I can't be here right now" I said

I ran back to the car, Steele followed directly behind me.

"If it's too soon then we can forget about the proposal" Steele said

The ride back was quiet. He didn't have anything to say nor did I. Mr. Busch took me to my house.

"Steele you ruined everything, you shouldn't have done that" I said right before I walked into the house.

"I guess I was wrong, we can take back the beach" Steele said

"Can we talk tomorrow?" I asked

"Yes, we can" Steele said

I ran into the house. Tears fell down my face faster than I could wipe them away.

All I knew in that moment was I needed to think about everything that happened that night. I loved Steele but marriage couldn't be real.

It's a lifetime commitment. I laid in my bed then fell right to sleep. I was done thinking about Steele's proposal. As soon as I woke up I knew I would need to talk to Steele. I knew exactly what to tell him so I did my morning routine. Showered, dressed, and makeup. I jumped in my car then drove straight to his house to tell him my answer. I figured out of respect I would tell him the answer in person. I knocked on the front door. I heard him running to the door.

"Skylan" Steele said

"Steele" I said

COMING SOON...

"We need to talk" I said

"I hope this is good news" Steele said

"Do you want to go for a walk?" I asked

"Yes" Steele said

He slipped his shoes on which was next to the door.

"Good" I said

Steele had a bunch of land so it wasn't limited to where we went but he had this little trail that I had been wanting to walk on since the first time I went to his house.

The trail itself was made of tiny pebble rocks with 30 feet tall trees that had green leaves on them.

"I just want you to know that I'm sorry for hiding everything from you. I thought I was doing the right thing at the time." Steele said

"I love you. I'm in love with you. You have been my crush since I was a little girl. So when I found out your history with my parents and my grandma..." I said

I looked at the ground while I closed my eyes. My eyes started to water.

"...it broke my heart. The love of my life. My childhood crush. He lied to me. It was more than I could fathom." I said

"It's understandable that you don't want to marry me." Steele said

"I do want to marry you. I just need a little bit of time to heal from everything. Right now just isn't the right time. I know you have pretty much put your life on hold for me. However, can you please just give me a little time? I want you but I just need time." I said

I knew I was asking more than I deserved but I needed time.

"So where would you like to go from here?" Steele asked

I knew I should have known that answer but being honest. I wasn't sure where to go from there.

"I'm not sure" I said

I didn't know what to say

"Umm" Steele said

Steele scratched his head with a little bit of confusion shown on his face

"Let's start with dinner" I said

"Ok I can do that" Steele said

"Tomorrow? 7" I asked

"Sounds good to me" Steele said

I took a deep breath and kept walking.

Steele took his hand then intertwined his fingers with mine.

The rest of the walk was quiet and peaceful. Not much was said but the emotions that were coming from both of us were memorizing.

Made in the USA
Monee, IL
22 November 2021

82706882R00108